The Con Artist's Takeover

The Mystery of the Unco-Nerdo School Teacher

CRIME STOPPER KIDS
MYSTERIES

Book Two

The Con Artist's Takeover

The Mystery of the Unco-Nerdo School Teacher

Karen Cossey

July 2019: Edition Two
First Print Version Published by: Stolen Moments (2018)
An imprint of Tui Valley Books Limited.
ISBN (Softcover): 978-0-473-45533-0

July 2019: Edition Two
Kindle Edition Published by Stolen Moments (2018)
An imprint of Tui Valley Books Limited
ISBN (Kindle): 978-0-473-45534-7

To Kate Gilmor
Thanks for encouraging me
to put some words to my dream
all those years ago.

Table of Contents

Who's Who (Character Glossary) ii
Chapter One: The Jump 2
Chapter Two: Painful Ugly Education 5
Chapter Three: Meeka's Home 14
Chapter Four: Motorbikes 22
Chapter Five: Brody Bankston and the Bet 33
Chapter Six: Sushi Mess 44
Chapter Seven: The Skimmer 54
Chapter Eight: Gillian's Plan 62
Chapter Nine: Jealousy 72
Chapter Ten: Breaking into Miss Cowan's 80
Chapter Eleven: Escaping Jungle Wars 88
Chapter Twelve: Miss Cowan Mystery 94
Chapter Thirteen: Breaking into Gillian's House 107
Chapter Fourteen: Waiting For His Turn 118
Chapter Fifteen: The Truth About Miss Cowan 125
Chapter Sixteen: The Truth About Meeka 131
Chapter Seventeen: All About Owen 142
Chapter Eighteen: Miss Cowan Mystery Explained 151
Chapter Nineteen: The Bugatti 161
Chapter Twenty: The Fireman 174
Chapter Twenty-one: The Jellybean Man 182
Chapter Twenty-two: Owen's Stories 192
Chapter Twenty-three: Chief Inspector Bankston.....................200
Chapter Twenty-four: Kidnap Threat 208
Chapter Twenty-five: Lia Castaneda Revealed 216
Chapter Twenty-six: Taken 225
Chapter Twenty-seven: Nate Fights Back 234
Chapter Twenty-eight: Sergeant Scary 243
Chapter Twenty-nine: Convincing Tessa To Stay 250
Chapter Thirty: Subconscious Mind 257
Chapter Thirty-one: Ninja Socks 266
Thank You For Reading! 276
Acknowledgements 277
FREE Book Box for You 278

Who's Who (Character Glossary)

Here is a list of people from the first book:
The Trespasser's Unexpected Adventure.

The Kids

Logan Seagate: Logan is a thirteen-year-old boy whose mother and younger sister died in a car crash when he six. Steve and Abby Kelly are his foster parents. He met Meeka and then they stumbled across and captured a group of gold smugglers. His father, Jake, was one of the gold smugglers who was caught and sent to prison. Logan loves motocross and rock climbing…or anything that gives an adrenalin rush.

Meeka (Dominica) Castenada-Whitley: As the daughter of a superstar singer and famous stunt coordinator, everyday rules don't apply to the overly imaginative, eleven-year old Meeka. Like Logan, she loves rock climbing and adrenalin.

Poet (Lauren) Parker: Logan's foster sister who is soon to turn twelve. Her mother died when she was born and on her seventh birthday, she saw her father murdered. She is quiet and observant, but stubborn and determined. She loves fashion and design. Cole Parker is her older brother and Steve and Abby Kelly are her foster parents.

Nate Kelly: Almost thirteen, Nate is Logan's best friend, and foster brother. He is always laughing and making jokes—he is the class clown. He loves Taekwondo and will be grading for his First Dan Black Belt soon.

Cole Parker: Cole is almost seventeen, Poet's brother and Logan's oldest foster brother. When he was twelve, he too saw his father murdered. He holds a First Dan Black Belt in Taekwondo. He also loves drawing and photography.

The Adults

Jason Whitley: Jason is Meeka's father and a stunt coordinator. Though sometimes his temper can flare, he is always quick to listen and cares deeply for Meeka and the kids.

Lia Castenada: Lia is a famous superstar singer who leads a very hectic life. She worries a lot about keeping Meeka safe and loves that Logan and his foster family are not fazed by her fame.

Steve Kelly: Nate's father, and the other kids' foster father, Steve, is a coast guard. He is calm and serious, and never loses his temper. He loves his foster kids as if they were his own.

Abby Kelly: Abby is Nate's stepmother and the others foster mother. She is a costume supervisor for the Theatre

Royal in Plymouth. She is artistic and creative and gets on well with Lia. She also loves the kids as her own.

Andrew Masterton: Andrew is Jason and Lia's best friend and bodyguard. He is also responsible for keeping a close eye on Meeka.

Mr Gomander: Mr Gomander was Logan and Nate's history teacher and the mastermind behind the gold smuggling. He wasn't caught by the police.

People You'll Meet in The Con Artist's Takeover

For your reference, here are some of the people from The Con Artist's Takeover who know Meeka or work at her home.

- **Gillian Tanner:** the household manager at Meeka's home.
- **Miss Cowan:** Meeka's teacher.
- **Walter:** The previous security guard at Meeka's, and her friend.
- **Frederick-Fish-Face:** the current security guard at Meeka's home.
- **Violet:** The previous cook who retired recently. She was also Meeka's friend.
- **Sofia:** Meeka's sixteen-year-old cousin who recently visited from Italy.

Chapter One:
The Jump

Midday Friday, last week of June, Spain.

The scream of police sirens kept coming as Andrew raced across the bridge in the Bugatti Veyron.

The police car was getting closer.

Up ahead was the dead-end drop into the river. The police car slammed on its brakes, but Andrew changed gears and sped up.

The sirens stopped. The only noise was the sound of the Bugatti's revving engine.

Would he make it? Andrew pushed the booster button as he hit the hidden ramp. Perfect timing. The Bugatti flew off the road, arched through the sky, then headed down towards the ramp on the other side of the river.

Great landing!

Andrew pulled the car to a stop.

Cheers erupted from the film crew as Andrew climbed out of the car and took his helmet off. Jason ran up to him.

"Wow! What a buzz. Did you see that?" Andrew waved his arm towards the river.

"We did. Got it all on film too. You sure know how to drive."

"Thanks, Jason. That was a blast. I never imagined a Bugatti could jump like that! Thanks for letting me have a go. I've been missing the Bug back home. Hey, maybe we should have it fitted out with a roll cage."

Jason rubbed his thumb across his fingers. "You want to pay for that? And all the repairs after the jump?"

Andrew looked at the car. The mechanics were shaking their heads.

"You're right." He smiled and tapped the car's bonnet. "I'll leave the stunt driving to the movie-makers."

Jason's assistant came up and passed Jason his mobile.

"Did she film it for you? Let's see," Andrew said.

Jason showed the video clip to Andrew.

Nice jump. That was going to be great on the big screen.

"You should send that to Lia," Andrew said. "Ask her if she wants to go for a drive."

Jason grinned at him and sent the message.

A minute later, his mobile beeped with Lia's reply. They looked at it together.

First time I've been glad the Bug's out of action. Love to go for a drive with you though. But let's take the BMW. A little more sedate for my liking. As long as Andrew's not driving.

Chapter Two:
Painful Ugly Education

9.30am Saturday morning, Cawsand, England.

Logan threw his helmet on his bed and headed downstairs to the kitchen. Saturday morning and he was starving. He'd been at the track since 5.30 practicing for next month's big race. The track was closing for the next two weeks so it had been his last chance.

Man, he was going to miss it. But he'd survive.

That thought made him stop at the kitchen door and scratch his head.

He wasn't as gloomy as he used to be, not since catching those shipwreck pirates. Thank goodness for Meeka, Nate and Poet. He had friends who were like family. Or was it family who were friends? Didn't matter. He was glad for it, both ways round.

"Have you seen Poet?" Abby asked as she pushed past him.

"I saw her lying on her bed," he said.

Nate came in from outside, sweating from a run.

"She was supposed to do her housework," Abby said.

"Mum, she's trying to break her record," Nate said.

"What record?" Abby asked and looked at them both.

Logan's heart skipped a beat.

"What record, boys?" Abby asked again, slower and louder this time.

Nate cringed.

Uh-oh.

"Popping bubbles. You know, on a bubble wrap popping app," Nate said.

"What! Whose pointless idea was that?" Abby asked.

Logan smirked as Nate's mouth dropped open. "I am currently the record holder for most pops. It's not pointless. It takes skill."

Logan snorted. Was Nate for real? Abby was not going to buy that.

"Well, it takes perseverance, a fine quality for anyone to develop. Plus it's on the tablet, so it's environmentally friendly. No wasted bubble wrap going out to sea," Nate said.

Abby groaned and shook her head. "Why did I ever let you guys have a tablet? So much for educational." She stomped out of the kitchen.

Logan looked at Nate and winked.

"This ought to be good," Nate said, grinning.

"Let's go see." Logan followed Abby upstairs. She was standing outside Poet's bedroom door, peering in. She turned to them as they came up to her. "How long has she been lying there?"

Nate checked his phone. "About two hours."

Abby sighed, then tiptoed into the room, sat on the edge of the bed and started rubbing Poet's lower back and bottom.

"Mum!" Poet turned around and sat up. "What are you doing?"

"Massaging your behind. Like they do to old people in hospital who can't move. If you lie on one side for too long, you need help to keep your circulation going."

"That's weird!" Poet jumped up and stomped out the room. The tablet dropped onto the floor.

Abby picked up the tablet. "I don't think she needs this any more." She headed off to her bedroom and came out empty-handed a minute later, before shutting the door behind her, and going downstairs after Poet.

Logan leaned against the wall next to Poet's door and looked at Nate who was laughing.

Another minute, and there should be some screaming from Poet.

"That's not funny!" Poet shouted from the bottom of the stairs.

Nate stopped laughing and turned to Logan.

"I found that funny. Did you find that funny?" Nate raised his eyebrow at Logan.

Logan wiped the grin off his face with his hand and frowned. "I found it hilari-arse."

Nate laughed again for a few seconds. "You know, you're getting a lot funnier since you met Meeka."

The smile dropped from Logan's face and he glanced up to the ceiling. "Can you keep a secret?" he asked.

Nate stared at him, both eyebrows raised.

"Okay, okay. Don't look at me like me that. The thing is, I am a lot more relaxed since we met Meeka. She's ridiculous. But it's not only her." He shrugged and looked around before staring at Nate again. "I guess I feel more at home. I think I'm starting to like having my own mum and dad."

Nate beamed like it was Christmas morning.

"Don't get carried away, Nate," Logan said. "I haven't promised to marry you guys or anything."

"Thank goodness. But don't let on too much."

"Why?"

"Because as soon as Mum figures out you're settling down, she'll start giving you more jobs around here."

So true. Sometimes she was so crazy about housework.

"Good point. I'll keep up some moody moments then. That always makes her look worried."

"Yeah, you do those well. You're a real glum-bum."

"That's not funny," Logan said. "Take it back."

"Or what?" Nate stepped closer, puffed out his chest, and stood on tiptoes.

Logan frowned. If anyone else did that, he'd freak out. Sucked that he was such a scaredy-cat after all his Dad had done to him. Good it was only Nate being stupid. Even when he helped Nate with his self-defence, Nate never hurt him.

"I'll keep your birthday present for myself," Logan said. "I can do with some new socks."

Nate rocked back on his heels and let out his breath. "Socks! Please tell me you've done better than that for me, Mr-I-got-a-dirt-bike-for-my-birthday."

"They've got ninjas on them," Logan said.

The doorbell rang.

"Jason! Andrew!" Poet screamed.

They raced down the stairs, Nate pushing in front. He was such a cheat.

"Nate! Logan!" Jason said and hugged them both. Abby came into the room, and Jason hugged her too.

"Let go of my wife, you scoundrel." Steve came in from the kitchen, smiling as he dropped his workbag on the ground. He shook Jason's hand. "What are you doing here?"

"Andrew and I are on our way home from Spain in the jet, and we wondered if we could take you all back with us. You said you were both taking a week off to get some things done around here, but wouldn't you rather come have some fun with us?"

Nate and Poet both yelled.

The jet! That would be wicked!

Steve and Abby looked at each other.

"What about painting the second floor?" Steve asked, eyebrows raised.

"The scaffolding guys can't come until Wednesday. What about building a wood shed?"

"I am kind of tired." Steve looked at Jason. "It's been a crazy month since Lia Castaneda was reported staying at Hideaway Lodge. You wouldn't believe how many sightseers get stuck by the tide when they're walking around the cliffs to the lodge. Maybe we could all take a few days off and come back by Wednesday for Nate and Poet's birthdays. The kids would only miss a couple days of school. I'm sure they can catch up."

Poet frowned.

Oh, yeah. She had her science project due next Friday— on her birthday. She complained about it a lot. But she wouldn't mention it now, would she?

"It would make Meeka happy," Jason said.

"Yeah, she needs cheering up. Her teacher's giving her a hard time," Poet said.

Phew. She wasn't going to say anything about her homework.

"You know about that?" Jason asked, eyebrows raised.

"Sure—iMessage," Logan said. "We all know about it. We have a group chat. We talk to each other every day."

"I know about the group. It's cool. Keeps her sane. But I didn't realise she'd talked about her teacher. Maybe it's worse than I think. I could do with your guys help to work out how horrible this new teacher is. Meeka's imagination is inclined to get away from her sometimes. I can't go firing teachers every time they give her more homework than she likes."

"So it's a visit with a mission," Nate said.

"A critical mission," Poet said.

"One of the world's most important people's happiness hangs in the balance," Logan said.

"That's nice you think so highly of Meeka, and she's definitely the most important person in the world to me and Lia, but I wouldn't say she was one of the world's most important people," Jason said.

"I wasn't talking about Meeka," Logan said. "I was talking about her teacher. Miss Cowan."

Jason rubbed his chin. "What?"

"Mum is always saying teachers are some of the most important people in the world. Them and motorbike mechanics."

Jason laughed.

"And if you fire her, she won't be very happy," Poet said. "Plus, it's not so easy to find a good teacher. We still haven't got a replacement for Mr Gomander. Learning history from a history teacher is a drag, but it's even worse trying to learn it from a PE teacher."

"So, can we go on this perilous mission into the jaws of painful ugly education?" Nate asked Abby.

"Ugly is the right word." Andrew cringed. "I don't know how Miss Cowan makes herself look so bad. She reminds me of a mean old principal who made my life miserable when I was at school."

"Don't judge a book by the cover," Nate said. "Don't worry. We can give an accurate opinion based on her teaching abilities. Some of my best teachers have looked hideous. Anyway, we're all used to having to look at Cole every day, yet we allow him to stay. Maybe because he's good at the dishes."

"I notice you say that while he's not here." Abby smiled, then turned to Jason. "We'd love to come, Jason. But you need to know I'm on Miss Cowan's side."

"That's good," Steve said. "Cole will get back from the gym in a minute. Then we'll have four kids in the house opposed to any form of education."

"That's not fair, Dad," Nate said. "Poet's been doing education on her tablet all morning."

Abby groaned.

Chapter Three:
Meeka's Home

Saturday 12.45pm, Wonersh, Near London.

Meeka twirled her pen in her fingers. Miss Cowan had taken away her iPad. And her phone. Even her calculator.

The woman was trying to starve her to death, one piece of technology at a time. Techno-Torture.

Saturday afternoon and she was sitting in a classroom, staring out her window at her climbing wall and doing the maths she'd avoided doing during the week. Her disappearing tricks may have earned her some free time then, but she should have thought about how manic Miss Cowan was to teach her maths.

For once she wanted to scream, 'I'm only eleven!' She usually told anyone who would listen that she was almost twelve, even though it was three months until her birthday. It was Poet and Nate's birthdays in a few days. She wanted to get away from Miss Cowan and Gillian and visit them, but no one was home to take her. Even Andrew had left a few days ago to drive a car for Dad in Spain. Stupid stunt cars. Why couldn't Dad stay home for once?

She sighed and looked at her paper. Trigonometry. Or Try-Go-Crazy-Up-A-Tree. Or Try-Go-Bathroom-Again. Or Try-Go-Sneak-Out-The-Door.

Meeka put her head on the table. She was so stressed even her words were leaving her.

"Focus, Dominica." Miss Cowan's voice was stern. She was sitting at her desk, reading a maths text book. A maths text book! Meeka was doomed to death by numbers.

"Where are you?" a voice called.

Dad? Meeka stood up so fast her desk pushed forward and tipped over, her chair toppled to the ground, and her books crashed in a pile. She didn't care.

She screamed out of the room so fast it could've caught on fire behind her.

"Dad!" She threw herself into Jason's arms. Her knight in shining armour was here! No more trig-o-yuk-ery! "I thought you weren't coming back for another week."

"Andrew did such a good job with the stunt, I made up some time, so I thought I should surprise you," Jason said. "Guess who else is here?"

Meeka swung around. It was her crew! Could life get any better?

"You're all here!" she said as she gave each of them a hug.

"Jason said we needed to come rescue you from your teacher," Nate said.

Logan coughed and nodded for Nate to look behind him.

Was Miss Cowan behind them? Poor Nate. Miss Cowan would probably turn him into a frog.

Meeka turned around and looked at Miss Cowan frowning at Nate. She was a short woman with big black framed glasses perched on a short nose that would've been cute on anyone else. On her it looked plain evil. Her dull black hair was pulled back in a high bun and she had a wart on the right side of her chin. She wore grey trousers and a plain white blouse with long sleeves, even though it was quite warm.

Maybe she didn't believe in showing her skin. Or maybe she had boils all over her arms. Or maybe her arms were made of snake scales. Or dragon skin.

Meeka couldn't wait to see what the others thought.

Nate shuffled his feet and looked down.

"Good afternoon, Mr Whitley," Miss Cowan said. "It's good to see you home. I know you want to go off and spend time with your family, but could I please have a quick moment of your time now?"

Meeka tugged on Dad's arm. He'd only just got home. He couldn't go and talk to this hideo-trocious woman now.

Jason looked down into Meeka's eyes. She opened them wide.

He sighed.

"Not yet Miss Cowan," he replied. "I still have to see Lia."

"Then I'll find you later," Miss Cowan said and turned and walked back to the classroom.

"Somehow that scares me," Meeka heard Jason whisper as he hugged her again.

Logan watched Miss Cowan leave, puzzled. He'd been facing the classroom when she'd appeared at the doorway. She'd stepped out of the room, leaned against the door frame and her shoulders had relaxed. And she'd smiled. He was sure she'd smiled a big smile.

Then she'd come towards them and her back had straightened and her smile had vanished. When Nate made his teacher's comment, her mouth had twitched, and he could've sworn there was a laugh brewing in her eyes. Then she pulled down her glasses and the transformation was instant. Her expression had become hard and stern. From ordinary ugly to scary ugly. Just like that.

There was something going on. He'd have to keep an eye on her. But that was going to be tricky when there was so much to take in. This place was amazing, from the entrance with an anxiety-causing security guard, to the tree-lined driveway winding through the park-like grounds. But the house blew his mind. He'd expected an old castle fancied up like Hideaway Lodge, but this was a modern mansion with four or five houses dotted amongst the surrounding trees.

He couldn't wait to see the garage.

Jason looked at his watch. "Lia will be home in a little while. Let's show them around, Meeka."

Meeka stood up straight and put her nose in the air.

Here comes the tour guide.

"What we have here is the Minder's Mansion, and schoolroom," she said. "Not as well kept as the rest of the estate, but then it's only home for the lowly staff."

Andrew threw a cushion at her. "Please don't call me your Minder. And it's not a mansion. It's my home. Behave yourself, Miss High and Mighty. None of that lowly staff nonsense. The staff around here are your family."

Meeka's shoulders drooped and she let out a sigh. "Well, they used to be," Logan thought he heard her mutter. Then she poked her tongue out at Andrew.

"I missed you too," Andrew said. Meeka gave him a hug.

"Okay, this is Andrew's home, where I spend a lot of time. It's the reason some people call me a tomboy. You'll notice there's nothing pink in here. Andrew has an allergy to pink."

She was right. Nothing girlish anywhere. All guy stuff wherever he looked. Nice.

"How come you spend so much time here rather than your own house?" Poet asked.

"Because my parents are so important I have to share them with the world. So they're away a lot. Andrew's not important at all, so I don't have to share him with anyone. He refuses to look after me in my house because of his allergy to pink. I have to hang out here, so he can make sure I stay out of trouble."

Andrew frowned. "Is that how you see it? The 'Andrew's not important' part?"

Meeka nodded, grinning from ear to ear.

"Jason offered me a job jumping off a skyscraper with no safety gear. It's starting to sound appealing," he said. "How about I show you guys around? Then Meeka can take you back to her place and stay there for the rest of her life."

The house felt warm and inviting, like there was no money spared in making it feel relaxing. The kitchen was big enough to park a couple of trucks in. Monster-trucks.

"Look at this walk-in pantry—it's bigger than my kitchen," Abby said.

"Never mind the kitchen," Nate said. "Check out the lounge. That's the biggest TV I've ever seen, and a bookcase full of video games." Nate tilted his head to read the game titles.

There was some other stuff Poet was going ga-ga about, but the TV and video games were all that mattered.

"Wow!" Nate shouted. "This game hasn't even been released yet! How did you get that?"

"It's not what you know, it's who you know," Jason said, smiling. "Someone has to test them."

"Looks like you'll know where to find Nate if he goes missing," Andrew said.

"He's going to be too busy with what I have planned," Jason said. "But don't worry, Nate. We'll have time for an epic battle night on the Xbox. You're probably going to lose. Just saying."

Meeka made a choking noise. "We'll see about that. Nate and I are going to anniha-death you."

"Sounds cool," Nate said and high-fived Meeka.

"Okay," Jason said. "No practising on the sly. Let's go up to the house and wait for Lia. You should come too, Andrew. We'll go in the back way, so we can avoid the pink."

"You guys are so mean." Andrew sighed and walked over to a cupboard. "I can do pink. Look."

He opened a door and revealed a walk-in cupboard full of girl's toys and Barbie DVDs. He sniffed and wiped an imaginary tear from his eyes. "These are from the good old days when Meeka wore pretty dresses and sat on the couch, playing with her dolls and watching Barbie with me. We know them all off by heart, don't we Meeka?"

"I will admit to nothing," she said.

"When she turned six she gave it all away for sword fighting and piano practice."

"Exact-aloot-ly!" Meeka said. "Put that pink stuff away, Andrew. It's bringing me out in a rash." She shivered and raced off down the hall. "Let's go through the garage. It joins Andrew's house to our place."

Chapter Four:
Motorbikes

Logan stood, merged with the floor, unable to move. It wasn't a garage—it was a warehouse. He counted ten cars. All expensive. Gazillion-pound expensive.

"Do you like it?" Meeka asked.

"Lollapalooza," he said, keeping his eyes on the cars.

Meeka laughed. "I knew you'd love it."

Jason nudged his shoulder. "Come see this," he said.

They walked past a mechanic pit and all kinds of equipment.

"Andrew likes building up cars. It's his thing," Jason said.

Logan looked back. Andrew was showing Cole and his foster parents a hot rod. He was way into it.

They went through a door and stepped into wonderland.

Motorbikes! So many amazing motorbikes. There was a Ducati Desmosedici, a MTT Turbine Streetfighter, a Suzuki Hayabusa, and even a Dodge Tomahawk.

Unbelievable!

"Come look at this," Jason said. "I've been collecting them for years. But this is my favourite."

He pulled a drop cloth off a bike.

"It's an Ecosse ES1 Superbike!" Logan shouted. "Monsta-cool! I have a poster of one in my bedroom."

Jason grinned. "I only got it recently."

Logan's jaw dropped open. "Isn't it worth like three million pounds?"

"It's three point six million dollars. Which is about two point nine million pounds."

"Aww, it's cheap then," Logan said never taking his eyes off it. "Can I touch it?"

"Sure," Jason said.

He reached out his hand.

"Watch it!" Jason shouted.

Logan's heart pounded.

Jason laughed and hugged him, then held his shoulders.

"I just wanted to make you jump. Go on, you can hop on it if you like. It's only a bike."

Logan let go of his breath and climbed on the bike.

Meeka stood a little way off, watching Jason hug Logan. A frown stomped on her mood. Dad had only been home five minutes and he'd forgotten her. Stupid bikes. Stupid Logan.

She sighed. Probably that wasn't fair. Logan was her climbing buddy. She could share her Dad with him. Right?

She was being silly. Best to go hop on the Ecosse behind Logan and pretend to be escaping from a fire on a superbike. That would be cool. No, it would be scary hot. Scot?

She smiled to herself. Her made-up words were slowly coming back. Things were going to be okay. Dad was home.

She went over and climbed on the back of the bike.

"What are you doing, Meeka?" Jason's forehead scrunched up. "Logan's on there. Hop off right now."

She slid off the bike and stared at Jason. "I thought we could pretend to be escaping a fire. It would be scot." Her shoulders sagged.

Jason let out a deep sigh. "Scot? Another new word, huh? Tell me later what it is. I'm going to take a photo of Logan on the Ecosse for his wall." He turned back to the bike.

Like she wasn't even there.

He'd always loved her new words. Not any more.

Not now Logan was here.

She turned and trudged back to Andrew.

Logan watched her leave. Should he go after her? Then Jason started pointing out things about the bike and everything else fell out of his mind.

He was sitting on an Ecosse ES1 Superbike. Wicked! Or scot. Whatever that meant.

"You look great on that bike, Logan," Jason said. "Let's get another picture of both of us." They posed.

This was a cloudburst of great!

"Let's go," Jason said looking around for the others. "We've not got much time before Lia gets back. Be great to surprise her."

Poet and the others raced through the big house. Meeka's house.

Meeka's mansion, more like it.

Must be cool having two homes. There'd always be somewhere to run away to. Especially when your mother was being annoying. Mum always expected her to be doing schoolwork or jobs.

Meeka's house was gorgeous. There were so many rooms, all of them decorated like something out of a magazine.

If only she could spend the rest of the day wandering through the house looking at things and taking photos. That would be bliss.

But Meeka seemed a bit quiet. It wasn't like her. How could she get Meeka to snap out of her mood?

"Come look at this, Poet," Abby said. She was standing in a doorway, gaping.

"What's she looking at, Meeka?" Poet asked.

Meeka sighed, gave a half smile, and pushed past. "Come see the pool." Meeka grabbed Poet's hand, pulling her along with her.

Wow! The pool was beautiful, large, and deep, if the kayak tethered in one corner was any way to judge. The view out the floor-to-ceiling windows was of a grove of trees. Potted plants filled the room. It looked like a jungle. This place was great!

"This water is so warm." Nate leaned over the pool and dipped his hand in the water.

"Isn't this amazing, Poet?" Abby asked her, smiling.

"Reminds me of Roald Dahl's poem." She looked at the pool. "You know, the one about not bathing in the sea and always using the swimming pool."

"The Shark," Abby said.

"That's the one," Poet said. "You remembered it."

"Of course. I pay attention to you," Abby said and squeezed her shoulder. "The shark sounds so scary in that poem, I'm surprised you ever go swimming in the sea."

"If I had this pool, I'd never have to. Anyway, I'm more scared of piranhas than sharks." Poet sighed. "Sorry about this morning. I forgot the time. I only meant to be on my tablet for five minutes."

"We're all good. Sorry if I embarrassed you."

"Nah, I guess it was kind of funny. Just don't do it again. It won't be funny a second time."

Abby smiled at her then looked around. "Don't you think this place is incredible?"

"It's a designer's dream," Poet said.

"Come this way, ladies!" Poet turned and saw Jason standing at the door, looking at his watch. The others had left.

"Let's go wait for Lia," Jason said.

Poet was sitting on the couch next to Meeka, and opposite Jason, when Lia walked in. She always looked so glamorous, even in jeans and a t-shirt.

Lia must have been warned they were there, because she winked at them over the top of Jason's head and put one finger to her lips before sitting on the couch next to him. She picked up a magazine from the coffee table.

He frowned, leaned forward then turned to her.

"Hi, hon," he said.

"Oh, you're here," she said. "Did you have a nice day? Did you remember the milk?"

He rolled his eyes to the ceiling. "Actually, I had a fantastic three weeks. And no, I didn't get the milk."

"Three weeks?" Lia let go of her magazine and stared at him. "Has it been that long? I could swear you only left this morning."

Jason sighed and stood up. "I'm going to go out of the room, come back in and try this again."

He took a few steps towards the door and Lia leapt up. "Don't leave! I couldn't bear it if you decided to stay away another three weeks!" She hugged him hard.

Meeka jumped up and joined in.

Lia came over and gave them all a hug, one by one.

"It's so good to see you," she said. "I missed you all."

She hugged Poet and whispered in her ear, "I need to talk to you later. Alone."

That was exciting.

They all talked for a while, catching up on each other's news. Well, most of them talked. Meeka sat, her mouth pressed shut.

What was her problem? Didn't she like having them there? Meeka was the reason Poet had wanted to come. She had so much homework to do. Okay, to be honest, who cared about homework when you could go for a flight in a jet? It was fabulous.

At the far end of the room, a door opened and in walked a well-dressed, good-looking woman. Poet had no idea who she was, but she looked like she belonged.

Did Andrew sit up a bit straighter? Did Meeka move a bit closer to Poet?

"Oh, you're back, Mr Whitley. Hello, Andrew," the woman said. "Welcome home." She smiled at Andrew and looked even lovelier. Like a princess. All the lady needed was a ball gown. Some expensive shoes would be good too. And fancy hair. Yes, she would definitely suit any of the ball gowns she had seen on Pinterest last night. Wouldn't it be nice to look that beautiful?

Poet glanced at Meeka. She still looked like she had eaten a sour lemon, but then she let out a breath and her face relaxed. But her shoulders still looked tense.

What was up with her?

"Thank you," Jason said. "Everyone, this is Miss Tanner, Lia's secretary and the person who keeps most things running around here."

"Please, call me Gillian. I've heard a lot about your family and seen lots of photos. It's nice to meet you all." She glanced at each of them in turn, but her eyes rested on Logan for a few extra seconds.

Logan looked at Poet and mouthed 'Code U'.

That meant he had his uneasy feeling. Best to listen to Logan's instinct.

Poet studied Miss Tanner. She seemed nice enough. But Meeka was sitting so close to Poet it felt like she was trying to hide behind her. Or maybe she was trying to disappear down the back of the couch. Something wasn't right. If she could get Meeka alone for five minutes, she'd tell Poet what was wrong. For sure.

"I'll leave you all to catch up," Miss Tanner said. "I asked Miss Cowan earlier to meet me here to go over some of Meeka's test results."

Meeka looked at the floor.

That must be her problem. Bad marks in her schoolwork. Strange that the secretary cared about that. And strange that Meeka would have bad marks. She was smart.

The door opened and in walked Miss Cowan.

"Hello again." She frowned at Miss Tanner. "Perhaps we should meet in my office now everyone has arrived."

"No, that's okay Miss Cowan," Lia said. "If you talk quietly over in the corner there, we won't even notice you're here. I need to see you in a few minutes anyway, Gillian."

What's Miss Cowan's first name? How come she's Miss Cowan, but Gillian isn't Miss Tanner?

They sat down near the far wall at a second set of expensive-looking couches and Miss Cowan pulled out some paperwork for Gillian to look at.

"This isn't it, Miss Cowan," Poet heard Gillian say.

"I haven't finished marking yesterday's test," Miss Cowan said.

Poet glanced over and saw Gillian frown. She looked … actually, she looked kind of scary. Gillian's mobile rang. "Yes … I'll be right there."

"Is everything okay, Gillian?" Lia asked.

"New staff," she said. "I'll sort it out and be right back. Maybe you could sit here and mark that test, Miss Cowan." Her voice was icy.

Miss Cowan pressed her lips together. Now she looked like a prune-face. Her wart wobbled. Was it in the centre of her chin now? Surely it had been more on the right before?

"Certainly, Miss Tanner," Miss Cowan said.

Logan moved and sat on Meeka's other side. He must be trying to keep an eye on Miss Cowan. Meeka moved away from him and even closer to Poet, almost sitting on her knee.

Did Logan smell? Or was it something else?

Chapter Five:
Brody Bankston and the Bet

Saturday, 1.30pm

Poet nudged Meeka trying to get Meeka to look at her so she could whisper, 'What's wrong?'

Meeka kept staring at her hands.

"It's good we've got Gillian to keep things ticking over," Lia said. "She's been here for a year now. She's a great help to us both."

Poet saw Miss Cowan let out a breath and shake her head slightly before she picked up a pencil.

"Tell us about your movie," Cole asked Jason.

"Can't tell you much. It's all being kept under wraps," Jason said. "But I can tell you a bit about Brody Bankston."

Miss Cowan dropped her pencil.

"Brody Bankston is great," Poet said.

Jason looked at her. "Aren't you too young to notice movie stars?"

"Nope," Cole said with a smirk on his face, "She's got a massive thing for him."

"I can't wait to see his new movie, Jungle Wars Two," Poet said. "It comes out today and we're going for my birthday. He was hot in Jungle Wars."

"Especially when he took his shirt off," Meeka said. She was smiling. Finally!

"Especially when he did that," Poet said and grinned at her.

The parents looked at each other and laughed.

"I don't get told I'm hot when I take my shirt off," Steve said.

Poet's face scrunched up. "Eww, Dad."

"Don't take your shirt off either, Dad," Meeka said shaking her head hard.

"I still like it when you take your shirt off, hon." Lia kissed Jason on the cheek.

"No, no, no." Meeka screamed. "Cut that out!"

"Why? I haven't had a decent kiss in ages," Jason said.

"Hope you haven't had any indecent ones," Nate said.

Everyone stared at him. Silly Nate.

Nate looked at the floor. "Oops. That kind of just slipped out."

Jason laughed and squeezed Nate's shoulder. "There's been no kissing, decent or otherwise."

He leaned over to Lia as though he was going to give her a kiss but then turned back and faced them instead. Lia's shoulders slumped.

"But that does remind me of what I wanted to tell you about Brody," he said. "We hit it off well. He's a fun guy, but sensible—except when it came to wanting to do his own stunts. He had a go at a few things. He got bruised all over, jumping out of a moving car, but I still had to almost tie him up to keep him from trying to do some of the more dangerous motorbike scenes."

Poet heard a snap and looked over to Miss Cowan. She'd broken her pencil in two. Weird.

"But there was one scene he begged me to find a stuntman for," Jason said.

"What was it?" Poet asked. "Running through a river of alligators?"

"Maybe sliding down a cliff into boiling mud," Cole said.

"Or parkouring from one flying old-fashioned aeroplane to the next," Nate said.

There he went, mentioning parkour. He never gave up. There was no way Abby would ever let him join the parkour class at the gym. Her friend's son broke a leg and both arms doing it.

"None of that," Jason said. "But I do like the airplane idea."

"You could combine it with the falling into boiling mud idea," Meeka said. "Maybe there could be alligators as well."

"Sounds like Brody. He'd be keen. But none of those were close to the scene he asked me to find someone to do for him."

"What was it?" Meeka asked.

"Kissing Olivia Bianchi," he said.

"No way," Cole said, his head jerking back. "Olivia Bianchi is drop-dead gorgeous. I love her movies."

"Now who has a thing for a movie star?" Poet said.

"Okay, okay, smarty-pants. But why would he not want to kiss Olivia Bianchi?" Cole asked Jason.

"Could have something to do with someone telling him Olivia was like a breath-sucking lung-deflating kiss python."

"You didn't?" Lia asked, shaking her head.

"Actually, I did. It was so funny. I told him she's an ex-Olympic swimmer, so she can hold her breath for ages and she can't help herself. She has to kiss a guy until he faints."

"Well, I'd faint if Olivia Bianchi kissed me," Cole said.

"Of course. But I told him that if you looked at her last two movies, the kiss scenes only show you the back or a tiny bit of the side of the guy because the hero kissing her was a stunt double. She's like a powerful human vacuum cleaner—she'll suck the life out of you. Then I told him both stunt doubles had ended up in hospital from suffocation."

"And he believed you? Why?" Abby asked.

Even Miss Cowan was smiling.

"I don't know why. But you should have seen him filming the kiss scenes. It was crazy. He didn't want to get near her. I know Olivia quite well, so I let her in on the joke and she played along with it like the great actress she is. You should have seen her taking deep breaths just before they were meant to kiss. Brody freaked out! She didn't tell him she knew about it until the next day." Jason was laughing as he wiped a stray tear from his eye.

"What happened when he figured out it was a joke?" Steve asked.

"He was mortified! He swore to get me back. Said something about enlisting his sister's help because she's an ace practical joker. He swore I wouldn't know what hit me."

"He sounds so mad," Meeka said. "I guess we won't ever get to meet him. He reminds me of someone, but I can't work out who it is. I wanted to meet him, so I could figure it out. It sucks that we won't be able to. It's kissucky."

Jason laughed. "No, he's all good. We're still friends. I invited him over, and he'll call when he's next in London. But he's still filming in Spain."

"That's better. It's kissappy," Meeka said.

"I wonder if he'll take his shirt off for you," Logan said, eyebrows raised and nodding his head at Poet.

Poet grinned.

"Probably not," Jason said. "We're shooting his third movie. It's nothing to do with jungles and he's glad about it. He's still not used to all the hype from Jungle Wars, and he's tired of everyone wanting him to take his shirt off wherever he goes. Said he might take a holiday in the South Pole so no one would expect him to bare his chest."

Poet thought Miss Cowan said something.

"What was that Miss Cowan?" Lia asked.

"Nothing," she said.

Gillian stepped into the room through a door next to Miss Cowan. "She said she could get him to take off his shirt."

"Really?" Jason said, covering his mouth with his hand. His eyes were as large as saucers.

"I was being silly," Miss Cowan said. "I was thinking he would be a good example of different muscles which we studied in anatomy a few weeks ago. I'm sure Mr Bankston would be happy to help if it was for education."

Poet pulled back a laugh, although she heard a few giggles around her. It was a strange thing to say. It was a good sign though that Miss Cowan could try and be funny, even if she was way off.

"Tell you what, Miss Cowan," Jason said. "If you have the opportunity, I bet you fifty quid you can't get Brody to take his shirt off."

Miss Cowan's eyes narrowed. "I was trying to be light-hearted, Mr Whitley. But I'll take your bet, to prove I can be a good sport."

"Done," Jason said.

"Lia, I need to see Meeka for a moment about her piano lessons," Gillian said.

"Is everything all right?" Lia asked.

"Nothing to concern yourselves with," Gillian said.

Meeka had a panicked look on her face. When Poet glanced over at Miss Cowan, she had the same panicked look, but then she shook her head and frowned.

"How about I come with you both and we talk on the way to my office. I can get the rest of Dominica's test for you while we're there," Miss Cowan said.

"You didn't bring it all? Isn't that what I said we were meeting about?" Gillian let out a breath. "It's all right, Miss Cowan. We can meet later."

"I think we should meet now, Miss Tanner," Miss Cowan said. "You can talk to Dominica while we're walking. I can go over the test with you in my office, and then you can get back to help Lia. Remember, it's important I'm kept in the loop with Dominica's piano lessons." She stood up. "Come on, Dominica. We'll only keep you for a minute. We both know how much you want to be with your family and friends."

Miss Cowan headed out the door so fast Gillian didn't have a chance to respond.

"Are you okay?" Poet whispered to Meeka. Meeka stood up, biting her fingernails.

"I wish my Guardian Pixie were here, that's all." She spoke quietly, almost to herself. Poet had to strain to hear what she said. Then she was gone, following the women out of the room.

"That Miss Cowan is very strange," Jason said.

"Gillian doesn't seem to like her," Lia said. "I've only been back a week, and she's complained about her three times. It seems she only wants to teach maths."

"Then why did she talk about anatomy class?" Abby asked. "Maybe Meeka needs extra maths tuition."

"I don't think so," Lia said. "She's already two years ahead of her year group. I'm beginning to think we'll need to find another teacher."

"Or Meeka could take a year off and come with me wherever I go," Jason said. "Like she used to."

"That would be great," Logan said. "She'd love that."

"If she's a couple of years ahead, surely it wouldn't hurt?" Steve asked.

"She could still do some work to keep up to date," Abby said.

"It's not that simple," Lia said. "Gillian thinks it better for Meeka to keep going with her schoolwork while she's doing so well. I wish she could come on tour with me too, but it's so hectic, I don't think it's fair on her. Better for her to be here with Andrew and Gillian and a proper routine."

"I hate routine," Nate said.

"That's why you're here now," Jason said, clapping his hands together. "Time for a change. I've got a few loose ends to tie up with my producer on the phone for an hour or so, but you guys should make yourselves at home. Try the rock wall or video games or go for a swim or a kayak. I did forget that Brody's premiere is on tonight. Thanks for reminding me, Poet. Lia and I should go, seeing as we're both back here in London. Would be wrong not to."

"Can we come?" Nate asked.

"Sorry, Nate. It's a red-carpet affair, so it's booked up. We were sent our tickets over a month ago. I'm sorry Steve, Abby."

"We'll be fine hanging out here," Steve said.

"Abby's always working behind the scenes at the theatre," Lia said. "How about I get you all tickets to a show, so she can actually sit and watch one? We could meet up for supper afterwards."

Abby smiled. "Sounds great. I'd love that."

It would be fun. Logan was cringing. Typical. He had no class.

"Or ..." Jason leaned over and pulled a DVD case from the coffee table drawer. "Steve and Abby could go to the show and you guys could stay here and watch the director's cut of Jungle Wars Two."

"Yes, please!" Poet shouted and jumped up. That would be so cool! Brody Bankston. He was soooo great.

"Good idea," Cole said. "The kids would love that, but I didn't get into Jungle Wars. Maybe I could go to the theatre with Mum and Dad?"

"You would've liked the movie if Olivia Bianchi was in it," Poet said. Typical Cole. Trying to act like a grown-up.

Cole poked his tongue out at her.

"That's fine with me," Abby said.

"Great," Lia said. "How about you three come with me and help decide what show to go to, then I'll make a couple of calls and we'll all meet back here in an hour. Abby, you and I will have to go to my salon to get ready. We can chat there."

"What a burden," Poet said.

Chapter Six:
Sushi Mess

Saturday 2.30pm

Logan followed Meeka to the climbing wall while Nate dragged Poet off to Andrew's house to play an Xbox game. Meeka didn't say a single word to him.

The rock wall was outside, but under a shelter and it had automatic belaying. It would have been tectonically great if Meeka hadn't been so grumpy.

"Bet I can beat you to the top," Logan said. Meeka hated losing.

She stared at him, like she was coming to some kind of decision.

Logan held his breath.

She smiled at him. Like old times.

"You'll never catch me. You can only go fast on a motorbike. You're like breakneck-dirt-bike-kid but you've got scooterfeet."

"I'll show you who's scooterfeet," Logan said.

They took off, racing each other up and down. At long last, he managed to beat her … if you didn't count his five second head start.

"Cheat." Meeka rubbed her arms. "Let's go see what the other two are doing."

Logan swung his arms around. "Okay. But it wasn't cheating. It was making the most of an opportunity."

Meeka huffed, turned, and started running. "Beat you to the garage then," she yelled back at him.

She won. Of course. But that was definitely cheating.

"Steve and Abby have gone for a walk." Andrew closed the bonnet of the BMW he was showing Cole. "Poet and Nate are taking a break from the game. Poet saw the sushi stuff I had out in the kitchen and wanted to make some. She tricked Nate into helping her, so he's not happy. We're keeping out of the way."

Uh-oh. This wasn't going to end well.

Andrew looked at Logan and stopped still. "Is there a problem?"

"Maybe not." Logan smoothed his hair down. "It's just that we have a house rule that Poet and Nate are never allowed alone together in the kitchen."

"Oh, yeah!" Cole said, frowning. "I forgot."

"Why?" Andrew asked.

How did Logan explain the mess that always appeared when Nate came up with some fun idea involving food and kitchen utensils?

"I have noticed Nate's not that great on monster-quenchers," Meeka said.

"She means consequences," Andrew said. "Childhood word she refuses to drop."

"Well, she's right. Nate and consequences don't often get put in the same sentence. His frontal lobe is definitely underdeveloped," Logan said.

"Bit like someone else I know." Andrew glanced at Meeka who smiled and shrugged. "Poet's sensible, though. I'm sure it'll be fine." Andrew looked relaxed.

"The problem is Poet has a hard time saying no to Nate, especially when he has one of his brainwaves," Cole said. "If Nate told her it was fun to skewer herself with a sword and pretend to be a roasted marshmallow, all she'd do is ask if she could be a pink one before he ran her through the middle."

Logan clutched his stomach and took a few staggering steps.

"Now I'm worried. Let's go." Andrew strode past Logan and Meeka into the house. Logan glanced over his shoulder and saw Miss Cowan coming towards them. Wonder what she wants?

"What a mess!" Andrew exploded when he saw the kitchen covered in wall-to-wall rice. Nate and Poet turned towards them. Nate put his arm round Poet's shoulders and pointed at the rice moustache stuck on her face. It went out across her lips then straight down to her chin.

"D'ya like Poet's moustache? She looks evil, huh?"

Andrew was staring at the walls with his mouth wide open.

Nate looked around and frowned. "Oh. Sorry, Andrew. We had a war. It was an epic battle."

"I see you've been cooking again, Mr Masterton." Miss Cowan stepped into the kitchen. "Perhaps you should consider taking a sushi class."

Now Andrew looked steamed.

"Very funny, Miss Cowan. I'm sure the kids will get it cleaned up in a minute. Won't you?" He frowned at Nate and Poet.

Poet took a step backwards and put her hand up to her face. Looked like she wanted to disappear.

"And no more cooking today," Andrew said. "That means absolutely no chocolate brownie cooking, Meeka. Not for the rest of the week."

"But how will we cook brownies for our chocolate brownie contest?" Meeka stared at him with her hands clasped in front of her. "We've been messaging each other for ages about it. We didn't get to do it last time we were all together. And I told Mum we'd make some for her."

Who could refuse her? She was practically begging.

"I'm sure you'll survive," Andrew said.

Woah. Tough guy. Impressive.

"How can I help you, Miss Cowan?" Andrew asked.

"Can I please talk with you for ten minutes, Mr Masterton?"

Andrew looked at his watch and shook his head. "Not now, Miss Cowan. I'm busy."

Miss Cowan's hands tightened into a fist. "Perhaps this evening then. It's important."

"I think today is out of the question, Miss Cowan," Andrew said, his back stiffening. "I'll try and make time tomorrow, but I think it would be best to wait until Steve and Abby have left."

Miss Cowan took in a deep breath. "Let's try tomorrow, Mr Masterton. It is important. I wouldn't waste your time when Dominica has friends staying."

She turned, but as she did, she wobbled on her high heels and fell against Andrew.

They both jumped back from each other like they'd been bitten by a snake.

"Sorry, Mr Masterton," Miss Cowan said.

"That's all fine," Andrew said.

Liar.

Miss Cowan turned and walked out. Not a single wobble in her shoes.

Meeka laughed. "You should have seen your face, Andrew! It looked like a camel had sneezed all over you!"

Andrew cringed. "That was scary."

"You should have talked to her. She won't give up. She never gives up," Meeka said.

"I know." Andrew bit his lip. "I was in a bad mood about the sushi. I didn't want to see her."

He sighed and looked over at the kitchen. "I guess I could help you clean up as my punishment for lying to Miss Cowan. Just please don't make me go talk to her today. She gives me the chills."

49

Poet felt awful. Why did she always let Nate talk her into doing dumb stuff? She didn't dare to look at Andrew while he and Cole helped her and Nate clean up the kitchen.

"I'll finish here," Andrew said. "Poet and Nate, you can play a game with Logan and Meeka. Cole, you better find your parents."

Thank goodness. She never wanted to go in a kitchen again. Especially with Nate.

Meeka and Nate were an awesome team at Xbox. They played for half an hour and Logan and Poet were getting thrashed. Thank goodness Lia turned up.

Logan shook his head as he dropped his controller. "I'm hungry."

"Not doing so well there, hotshot?" Lia smiled at Logan and then winked at Poet. "Never mind, it's time for a snack."

"You're always having snacks Mum." Meeka rolled her eyes. "Have you guys seen how much my Mum eats?"

"I have noticed that," Logan said, "I thought beautiful superstars were always on diets."

Nate shook his head, mouth downturned. "We had nothing to eat for a week after her last visit. Mum used up all our summer supplies feeding her."

Poet threw her arm round Nate's shoulder and matched her expression to the tragic look on his face. "We had to ask the local orphanage for food."

Lia laughed out loud. "Talking about food, I'm here to judge your chocolate brownie competition. What happened? I don't smell anything, and I'm desperate for some chocolate."

Nate looked down at his feet. Poet examined her fingernails. They needed trimming.

"Let's say they're banned from the kitchen for a while," Andrew said. "I'll tell you about it later. I may be able to find some chocolate brownies in the freezer if you're lucky. I made some before I went away with Jason."

Andrew disappeared and came back a few seconds later holding a plastic container.

"Here they are." He opened the lid. "There's nothing here. Meeka, did you take these?" He waved the empty container in Meeka's direction.

"No, Andrew. Promise."

"Meeka, I don't mind you taking them, but I do mind you lying about it," Andrew said. "You're the only one who would take them."

"I agree," Lia said.

"I'm not lying! Don't blame me—I didn't take them," Meeka shouted, glaring at them both.

They shook their heads.

Odd. Why didn't Lia and Andrew believe Meeka?

"You don't trust me anymore!" Meeka turned and ran outside.

"Sorry Andrew," Lia said. "I don't know what's got into her lately."

"She doesn't usually lie outright. She'll make up a story, but she doesn't lie-lie," Andrew said, and then looked at his watch. "Sorry, I have to go. I have a meeting about the air show. I won't be back until late."

He headed for the garage, but then came back.

"Has anyone seen the keys to the BMW? I'm sure they were in my pocket."

Everyone looked around the room for a few minutes.

"Weird," Andrew said, looking at his watch. "I might have to take a different car."

"Here they are!" Nate called out, appearing from the garage. "They were on the workbench."

"Thanks, Nate." Andrew ruffled Nate's hair. "Appreciate that. Not enough though to ever again let you cook in my kitchen." He smiled at Nate and left.

Lia's phone beeped. "It's Gillian. She's got Abby with her, ready to go with me to the salon. Jason's taking Steve out for a catch-up and is going to drop Cole at an art supply shop he wants to visit. Then we'll all be back for dinner before we go out again tonight."

Poet smiled. Cole could spend days in a shop like that. Bet the London ones were huge. He'd be in such a good mood when he got home.

Lia glanced towards the door Meeka had run out and frowned. "I better go too, but I sure hate leaving Meeka like this."

"Don't worry. We'll get to the bottom of it," Poet said.

A slight smile settled on Lia's face. "All right guys, report in at dinner time. Meeka will show you where. Thanks for coming to stay. It's great to have you here. Meeka needs some friends right now. Sorry for the upset about the brownies. Tell Meeka we're going to forget all about it. I would have stolen them too if I knew they were there. Andrew makes the best brownies."

"Okay," Logan said. "Come on, guys. Let's find Meeka."

Good idea. Something was definitely wrong with her. What was going on?

Chapter Seven:
The Skimmer

Saturday 3.30pm

Logan spotted her first, high up a tree across the driveway. He'd have never seen her if he hadn't been searching. What a great hiding tree.

"Meeka. Come down!" he called out.

"I didn't take them," she shouted as she climbed down.

"Whoa, we believe you," Logan said. Sensitive!

"Yeah, it's only chocolate brownie," Nate said. "It wouldn't be worth being called a liar about."

"So who did take them?" Poet looked at Nate, her eyebrow raised.

"No way. I've only been here five minutes. I'm not going to raid Andrew's freezer. Have you seen him handle a gun?"

They all laughed.

"Come on, Meeka, what's going on?" Logan asked. "You seemed stressed when Gillian came in earlier. What did she want to talk to you about?"

Meeka turned her head away from them and mumbled.

"What was that?" Poet asked.

Meeka took a deep breath and faced them again.

"She only wanted to talk about my piano practice. Nothing really," she said.

She gave them a big smile. A stack of fake! She was definitely lying.

Logan stared at her, willing her to tell them the truth.

A courier van drove past them and Meeka turned to look at it. A woman hopped out and left a package at Andrew's door.

"Strange, someone coming at this time on a Saturday," Meeka said. "Walter would never have allowed it."

"Who's Walter?" Poet asked.

"Our last security guard. Andrew's in charge of security, and Walter worked for him. He was so much fun," Meeka said and shook her head.

"What happened to him?" Logan asked.

Meeka looked down at her feet. What was wrong with her? She looked miserable.

"Can we not talk about it right now?" Meeka looked like she could cry.

"Sure," Poet gave her a hug. "If that's what you want."

She had to be kidding. Logan needed to know what was going on. It was awful, seeing Meeka so upset.

"Come on, Meeka. You can talk to us. We're worried about you," Logan said.

Meeka sighed. "It's only that Walter made a mistake and Gillian told Andrew he should fire him. I don't think he would have fired Walter, except Andrew was so distracted. It's the same every year about this time."

She wiped her eye.

What kind of mistake got someone fired? Why wouldn't Meeka say? She was hiding something. But she still looked like she could cry, so maybe Poet was right. Best to change the subject. For now.

"Why was Andrew distracted?" Nate asked.

"His wife and daughter died in the Underground bombing thirteen years ago about this time," Meeka said.

Nate's jaw dropped. Poet had both her hands on her face, with her mouth open wide.

"Emma, his daughter, would've been fourteen this year." Meeka sighed again. "Every year about this time he tries to keep busy so he doesn't have to think about it. Usually he goes away for a few weeks, but this year he's helping organise a nearby air show. So he's still here, but it takes a lot of time. That's where he is most nights, at some meeting."

Logan's brain was spinning. How could this be? Andrew seemed to have everything. He looked like Captain America, and Poet went ga-ga over him even more than Brody Bankston. He had a great job, and a great home. And he was skilled with a gun like a super spy. He was the best, just what Logan would like to be one day. But he would never wish anyone to lose their family, their wife and child. That was the worst thing anyone could go through. He knew. He'd trade anything to have his mother and his sister back.

"He never lets on," Poet said. "He's never even mentioned his family."

"He doesn't talk about himself. He's always looking after everyone else," Meeka said.

Now Poet looked like she could cry. She understood the losing your family thing. She missed her father every day.

Logan let out a long breath he hadn't realised he'd been holding.

Blown up in the Underground. Unbelievable! He'd think more about that later. If something was wrong with Meeka, he needed to figure that out. It was important she was safe.

"So, Andrew's too busy for you, your favourite security guard is gone, and your teacher sucks. What about Gillian?" Logan asked.

Poet took her hand off her mouth. "She seems nice."

Meeka glanced at Logan. Was that fear in her eyes?

"She's all right I guess," Meeka said. *Lying. Definitely lying.* "It's all fine now you guys are here."

Now she was trying to change the subject.

"We're going to have some fun," she added.

"Hang on. Who's the Guardian Pixie you mentioned earlier?" Nate asked.

Meeka went red.

"Did you hear me say that?" she asked.

"Yep," Nate said.

"So did I," Logan said.

"That's nobody. An imaginary person I made up when I was younger," Meeka said.

Was that a lie?

"Hey, the courier left the package by the door," Meeka said. "Andrew won't be home until late. We should take it inside for him."

Okay, the subject was changed. Logan glanced at Nate, who nodded in Poet's direction. She'd probably get more out of Meeka later. They were always telling each other secrets.

They walked over and took a look at the box the courier had left. It was addressed to Miss Cowan.

"She gets parcels once a week at least. I think she buys a lot of stuff online." Meeka turned the box over. "Says it's a vacuum cleaner. Maybe Miss Cowan wants to test out her suction kissing ability like Olivia Bianchi."

Poet grasped her own neck with both hands and took a few staggering steps backwards.

Logan shivered. "Yuck. Surely no one's ever kissed Miss Cowan."

Meeka lifted one end of the box. There was a tearing sound and the vacuum cleaner slid out.

"Uh-oh. Vac-a-Wreck," Meeka said.

"You can do better than that," Logan said. "How about Oops-a-Cuum?"

Meeka grinned. "I'm just warming up. I've been out of practice. I need a suck-o-snake to clean out the pois-o-maths Miss Cowan's been pouring in my head."

She picked up the vacuum hose and pressed the end to her ear.

A panel on the top of the body of the vacuum cleaner fell off.

"Hey, this wasn't on properly." Nate picked up the panel and leaned over the vacuum cleaner.

"Funny. There's no insides in this vac-a-wreck," he said.

"Huh?" Poet asked.

Meeka squatted down and looked inside, pulled out a cardboard box and opened it. Inside was a thin piece of plastic with markings on it that ran into a wire strip and then onto two electronic green boards, with some attached wires. Nate pulled out what looked like an instruction sheet.

"What's this for?" Meeka asked.

"It's a 'Point of Sale Modification Device Kit'," Nate read.

Poet picked up the thin piece of plastic. "This part looks like it would fit over a cash machine. You know, over the pin-pad part."

"It's a credit card skimmer," Nate said. "It says so here." He pointed to a paragraph in the instructions.

"Oh, no." Logan bent over the vacuum cleaner and pulled out a small rectangular package. "Guess what this is," he said as he opened the package.

"Credit cards," Meeka said.

"Bet they're blank," Poet said. "You install this skimmer thing and collect people's credit card numbers, and then make up fake cards with their stolen numbers to go and use yourself."

"You could get lots of money out of a cash point machine that way," Nate said. "And you could buy stuff online too."

Poet was right. The credit cards were blank.

"What's Miss Cowan doing with a credit card skimmer?" Logan asked.

"Nothing good," Poet said.

"I can't believe she would have anything to do with this," Meeka said. "She's a real pain about maths, but she's actually decent most of the time. She can even be funny sometimes. And she always seems to know when ..."

"When what?" Logan asked.

"Nothing," Meeka said.

There she went, shaking her head again. She was hiding something.

"We've got to tell someone," Nate said.

"Tell someone what?" asked a women's voice behind them.

Gillian.

He hadn't seen her coming. None of them had seen her coming.

Gillian looked down at the vacuum cleaner and took the credit cards from Logan's hands. Her shoulders rose, like she was taking in a breath. Was she scared?

Chapter Eight:
Gillian's Plan

Logan saw Meeka's eyes jolt open wide as her face went pale. She was afraid, for sure. Why?

He turned his attention back to Gillian and explained how they had found the skimmer stuff in Miss Cowan's vacuum cleaner.

"This is serious. Very serious. Let's take it to my place," Gillian said.

Gillian's house was on the opposite end of Meeka's mansion to Andrew's. There was plenty of girl stuff in the big comfortable sofas, soft lighting, and classy pictures on the wall. It felt like a safe place to curl up and go to sleep. It felt like a home should feel. Logan hadn't felt that anywhere else in Meeka's place. So why was she biting her nails?

Poet walked over to the floor-to-ceiling windows.

"Wow, you have a view of the whole valley,' she said. "Come look at this, Logan."

She had stepped out onto a balcony and was pointing at a huge telescope.

Neuron-Blasting! Logan had always wanted a telescope like that. "You must love the stars to have such a massive telescope." Maybe Gillian was all right after all.

She sort of squirmed. "Of course. But let's go inside now. Best Miss Cowan doesn't see you here."

Gillian offered them all some juice, then sat them down.

"I don't want you to say anything about this to anyone," she said.

"You've got to be kidding!" Meeka yelled. "We've got to tell Mum and Dad."

"Especially not them." Gillian stared at Meeka and spoke slowly. "We don't want to worry them about anything, do we Meeka? It's not fair on them when they have such little time at home."

Meeka's eyebrows came together and she bit her lower lip. "I guess not," she said, shaking her head.

"Good." Gillian let out a breath. "I'm going to talk to Frederick, our new security guard, and get him to keep a watch on Miss Cowan. With his help, we should be able to catch her red-handed when she passes this skimmer onto whoever is next in line to receive it."

"Are you going to give the skimmer back to her?" Nate asked, his eyes wide.

"Of course," Gillian said. "I'll also notify the police, but the last thing we need is them coming here and causing a scene. It could ruin Lia's career if the media got a hold of this and made up a story about credit card fraud. Let's keep it to ourselves and have Frederick sort it out. Do we all agree?"

They looked at each other. The last thing Logan wanted was trouble for Lia and Jason. Poet and Nate both had their fists on their mouths. They must feel the same.

They all nodded to each other.

Gillian might have a good plan, but there sure was something strange going on between her and Meeka.

They left Gillian's house and walked back to Meeka's mansion.

"Do we have to keep this a secret from Mum and Dad?" Poet asked.

"Yes, we do!" Meeka was shouting.

"What's got into you, Meeka?" Nate asked. "You seem upset all the time."

"Of course I'm upset. My maths teacher is a crook and I have to keep it a secret!"

They all stopped walking and stared at her.

"Sorry, guys. I shouldn't yell, but I hate not being able to do anything about it."

"Who said we couldn't do anything?" Nate asked. "Why don't we do a little bit of detective work ourselves? You know, unless you want to keep yelling and blow the whole secret."

Logan laughed. "Meeka, what's going on between you and Gillian?"

Meeka stared at him and went pale. "I can't talk about it. Please don't ask, Logan."

Poet nudged him and gave him a telling look. All right, he'd leave it to her. But he wasn't happy about it.

"How about we break into Miss Cowan's house and go through all her stuff until we find something else that proves beyond a doubt she's a wicked evil criminal?" Poet asked.

"Sounds like a magnifibang-astoundamungus plan to me," Nate said, smiling at Meeka.

Those were Meeka's favourite words. Surely she'd snap out of her mood?

Meeka kept looking at Logan.

She was waiting for him to drop the Gillian thing. All right. He'd move on. For now.

"What do you think, Logan?" Meeka asked after he stopped staring at her.

"It'd be torqued-to-the-limit-cool," he said. "Let's go after dinner when everyone else has gone. If she's out, that is."

Saturday, 6.30pm

They walked up the stairs to dinner. Meeka almost tripped over Poet, who was gazing at the staircase.

Funny. Meeka had never really noticed the staircase before, and she ran up it every day. It was only a staircase. Okay, maybe it looked amazing, the way it curved like a wave with the wooden panelled ceiling wrapped around it. She'd never liked it because the glass sides were too difficult to climb. And the cleaners got mad when she tried.

Now Poet was mumbling.

"What's that?" Meeka asked.

Poet laughed. "Miss Cowan going out tonight got me thinking of that William Hughes Mearns poem."

"What poem?" Logan asked.

"Yesterday, upon the stair

I met a man who wasn't there

He wasn't there again today –

I wish, I wish he'd go away."

"Who do you want to go away?" Steve asked, from the top of the stairs.

"No one," Meeka said as Logan, Nate and Poet echoed her.

Steve stopped walking and looked at them with squinty eyes.

"It was only a poem, Dad." Poet ran past him. "You look great in that jacket, by the way."

"Thank you, Poet," Steve said.

"What about me, Poet?" Cole asked, coming over to them and doing a spin.

Nice outfit. Mum must have taken him shopping.

"Woah! Is that you Cole? Wow, you look like a movie star," Poet said. "Olivia Bianchi, eat your heart out."

Cole beamed and gave her a hug.

Poet sure knew how to say nice stuff. Maybe Meeka should talk to her about her problems.

Abby and Lia walked in.

Wow. Abby was diamond-tiara-dazzling. Who'd have known? None of her kids, given the way they were gaping at her.

Steve laughed.

"Look at you all, staring at Mum," he said. "Now you see her the same way I do every time I look at her. Entrancing."

Abby kind of melted and Steve kissed her.

Meeka looked at Poet and they mouthed "Gross" to each other. They should definitely talk later. Except Poet would tell Logan and then he'd be so upset. What if he stopped talking to her? He'd probably side with her Dad. Jerk. She better keep the secret to herself.

They all moved into the dining room, where they were served by the new cook, who was uptight and awful. Upful? Tightaw? Tight jaw? Tightful-spiteful. Nothing like Violet, their old cook. Meeka sighed.

"What happened to Violet?" Jason asked when the cook left.

"Gillian thought we should let her retire," Lia said. "She said she would keep on cooking for us forever, but it was better for her to have time for her family at her age."

"I thought she considered us her family as well."

"I know, hon. I was upset about it too. But in the end, Violet left while I was on tour. Not even a goodbye, only a note. Maybe we weren't so important to her after all." Lia sniffed.

Was Mum going to cry about it now? Bit late wasn't it? All crying would do was create some major make-up disaster on her face.

Jason reached over and squeezed Lia's hand.

"That's not true, Lia. You know she loved us as much as we loved her. We'll invite her back for dinner in a few weeks. Then we can say goodbye properly."

Lia sniffed again. "That'll be good. I do have to say this new cook is amazing. Wait until you try her dessert."

"I'd still rather have Violet," Meeka said.

"Can we go for a ride in the Bug tomorrow?" Logan asked.

"Didn't you tell them, Meeka?" Lia asked.

"Nope," Meeka said, looking down at her dinner plate. Not the Bug. Please don't make her talk about the Bug.

"Oh no," Lia said. "Why not?"

"I didn't want to upset them," she mumbled into her potatoes.

Lia and Jason looked at each other, frowning.

Lia coughed. "The problem is the Bug was stolen a few weeks ago."

Nate's knife and fork clattered on the floor. "Not the Bugatti Veyron!"

"How could it be stolen? From here?" Logan asked. "You've got security cameras all over the place."

"And I thought it was impossible to just walk in and take a supercar," Poet said. "You have to have the key, or the...what's it called? The key fob. You have to have the key fob, don't you?"

"Very good, Poet," Jason said. "There's not much point stealing a car like a Bugatti because the computerisation means it's easy to track. No, whoever took it only wanted to go for a joyride. And then they crashed it not far from here. It's going to cost the insurance company two hundred and fifty thousand pounds to get it repaired. It's back at the Bugatti factory now."

Two hundred and fifty thousand pounds. Did he have to bring that up?

"It must have been pretty messed up. Was anyone hurt?" Logan asked.

"No. No one was there when it was found. And it's not too much damage. They are super expensive to fix, that's all."

"Crazy." Cole was shaking his head. "Didn't your cameras catch anyone stealing it?"

"They would've if they'd been switched on, but Walter, our security guy, was upgrading them because there have been about ten cars stolen in the valley over the last six months. So, our cameras weren't working."

"I still don't think it was right to sack him over it," Lia said.

"Me neither," Meeka said. "He was my friend."

"We've been over this. It was Andrew's call. He's in charge of security," Jason said.

"Well, he only wants to keep Gillian happy," Meeka said.

"Sorry, everyone." Lia sighed, loudly. "The whole thing has been a nightmare. We all miss Walter, but Gillian was adamant he should go and she does have quite an influence over Andrew."

"Are you okay, Meeka?" Abby asked. "You look like you could cry."

Chapter Nine:
Jealousy

"I miss Walter, that's all. And Violet." Meeka wiped her eyes with the back of her hand.

"Come on, Meeka," Jason said. "Don't spoil the night for your friends."

Meeka took a short breath. Don't spoil it for Logan, he meant. Look at him now, smiling at Logan. Andrew had said the staff were her family. Well, her family had left, and Dad expected her to just forget about it and make do with Logan and Nate and Poet, who would only be here for a few days. What was she supposed to do for family next time she was alone while he was off making a movie somewhere? He wouldn't care, as long as could message Logan every day with stunt stories. Logan had shown her some of his messages. He didn't message her nearly so often.

Jerk. She was glad his stupid Bugatti was damaged. It should've been totally wrecked. Bet he'd be more upset about that than having to leave her alone with Miss Cowan and that Gillian witch.

Lia reached over and squeezed her hand.

"Of course you're upset, hon," she said. "No one likes to say goodbye to a friend."

That was too much. Meeka jumped up and ran out of the room.

"Get back here young lady," Jason called after her.

He could go jump. Out of a tall building. With Andrew.

Meeka stopped.

She'd never thought anything like that about Dad before. What was happening?

It was all Logan's fault.

She started running again.

Logan stood up. So did Jason.

Was Jason going to go after her? He should. He'd upset her with his stupid 'Don't spoil the night for your friends' comment.

"Sit down, both of you," Lia said. "Let her have some space for a few minutes."

Bad idea.

"Why's she so upset all the time?" Logan asked as he sat down.

Lia shrugged. "I'm not sure, but Gillian says she's been upset ever since Sofia left. Sofia filled her head with all sorts of stories about how great boarding school is. Gillian thinks she's suffering from a case of the grass is greener on the other side of the fence."

"Who's Sofia?" Steve asked.

"Keep up, Dad," Nate said. "Sofia's her sixteen-year-old cousin from Italy who came to stay after she got back from our place."

"Meeka didn't like one thing Sofia said about boarding school," Logan said. "At least, that's what she told us."

"I've always said there'd be no boarding school," Jason said. "I hated it."

"Maybe she's ready for some kind of change," Lia said.

"It's been enough of a change this year, keeping her at home rather than taking her with me on location. It was supposed to help her be settled. Not upset all the time."

"She seemed to be happy and settled earlier this year, staying home and not travelling so much," Lia said. "It's only the last few months she's been getting more uptight every time I'm home."

"Whatever you do, don't send her to boarding school," Poet said. "She'd loathe it!"

Logan ran both hands through his hair and held them on top of his head. This was ridiculous. Sitting here talking about Meeka. Why doesn't anyone ask her what's wrong?

"I'm going to go see her," he said.

"Me too," Poet and Nate said together.

"Let me go first," Jason said.

Finally! Common sense.

Someone coughed from the door. It was Gillian.

"Sorry, there's no time, Jason," she said. "You need to leave right now, or you'll be late to the movie premiere and Abby and Steve's theatre show starts soon."

"What? But—" Jason looked towards the door.

Did Gillian always appear when you didn't want her to?

"We've got this." Logan pushed past Jason, stopping at the door to wait for the other two.

"Don't worry Jason," Poet said, touching his arm. "It'll all work out."

"Send her a text from the car," Nate said as he went out the door. "Tell her you love her and all that nonsense. Girls like that."

"Am I taking parenting advice from a twelve-year-old?" Logan heard Jason say as he stepped out of the room.

"I'm thirteen on Wednesday!" Nate shouted.

"Well, that's all right then," Jason shouted back.

They ran outside.

"She'll be up the tree," Nate said.

"How do you know?" Poet asked.

"There's a platform up there you can sit on and see everything without being seen. It's the coolest hiding place."

"You climbed it?" Logan asked.

"Of course, scooterfeet. I believe in real-life climbing. Not this wimpy wall climbing. Automatic belays. Huh. Ridiculous."

Logan stopped. "You've been doing parkour, haven't you?"

Nate squirmed. "I may have been to a couple of classes. The instructor let me join in for free. I couldn't say no."

Logan laughed. "Everyone's got secrets. What about you Poet?"

"Can't tell you. It's a secret." Poet smiled at him.

They reached the tree. "Come on down, Meeka. We know you're there," Poet called out.

"Go away!" Meeka yelled back.

"Was that, 'go away' or 'come up'?" Nate asked.

"Definitely 'come up'," Logan said. He scrambled up the tree and made it to the platform. Nate followed. It was deadly good up there.

"Is there room for me?" yelled out Poet.

"Get up here, Poet. Don't leave me alone with these guys!" Meeka yelled.

Poet swung up the tree like a monkey.

"Poet, you've watched Jungle Wars too many times," Meeka said.

Poet turned to Meeka. "I know. Been practising some of the scenes in gym class. What's happening with you?"

"Nothing. I wanted to be by myself, that's all. I'm not used to having people around all the time," she said.

"Don't you want us here?" Nate asked.

"I don't mind Poet being here." She stared at Logan, her eyes slit.

Silent. Cold.

Felt like when his father had said nasty things to him. Logan's hands shook.

"Let's go then, Logan," Nate said. "We've got a house to break into. You girls enjoy your movie. Maybe you can count how many times Brody takes his shirt off."

Logan followed him down and walked with him to the trees outside Miss Cowan's house.

"Take a deep breath, Logan," Nate said. "Remember what your counsellor said about letting those thoughts go. Let what Meeka said go."

"How'd you know what I'm thinking about?' Logan asked.

"Your hands shake whenever you're remembering something bad about your father. Meeka is nothing like your Dad, so let that thought leave, okay? I think she's jealous."

"Jealous?" Logan asked. "Why? Look at everything she has. Look at who she is."

"Look at Jason giving you all the special attention. Showing you his bike. Telling her to hop off while you were on. Giving you a personal guided tour with his arm around your shoulder. Taking photos of you and him. When was the last time Meeka saw her Dad?"

"When she was with us. Three weeks ago."

"That's a long time in Meeka-land. Imagine being here for three weeks by yourself with a whole lot of strange new staff hanging around. You're so in raptures over Jason, your great hero liking you, you can't see what's going on. Her dad has hardly spoken to her since he got back, but he's made a point of talking to you plenty of times."

Of course, that was it. He should've seen it.

"You're only a twelvie. You can't know this stuff," Logan said.

"I've got eyes in my head. And I'm almost thirteen, remember?" Nate said.

"So you keep telling me. You must be looking forward to your Ninja-socks present."

"Ha ha. Hey, there goes Miss Cowan." Nate pointed at the house.

Miss Cowan came outside holding something that looked like a cake tin. There was no way it could hold a skimmer.

She climbed in to her car and drove away.

"Let's do this," Nate said.

"Okay, Nate," Logan said. "Hey, Nate?"

Nate turned back to look at him.

"Thanks," Logan said.

"Just get me something better than socks, please," Nate said as he walked away.

"But they've got cool Ninjas on them. You'll love them."

Chapter Ten:
Breaking into Miss Cowan's

Saturday 7.30pm.

Meeka stayed on the platform, hugging her knees. She pushed a tear off her face with the back of her hand. She shouldn't have said that to Logan.

"Meeka, that was mean," Poet said. "Why did you say that?"

"I dunno." Meeka looked away from Poet.

"You know, you don't need to be jealous of Logan."

Meeka sniffed.

"Your dad is nuts about you," Poet said. "He's always talking about you. The whole reason he asked us to come visit was because he's worried about you. He wanted us to check out Miss Cowan and see if we thought she was bad for you."

Meeka turned her head towards Poet. "Really?"

"Yes, really. He loves you," Poet said. "You should have seen him on the jet, showing everyone your stupid baby photos. Who keeps their kid's photo album on a jet plane?"

"He has copies of my album all over the place." Meeka smiled.

Her phone buzzed.

"It's Dad." She read the text, and smiled even more.

"What'd he say?" Poet asked.

"Hi sweetheart. I'm sorry I haven't spent any time with you since I got back. It's nice having your friends here but I miss you. I love you. Can we please have some time to ourselves tomorrow?"

Meeka beamed and texted Jason back:

YES PLEASE

"See," Poet said.

"I better go and say sorry to Logan."

"Good idea."

"Uh-oh." Meeka pointed down to the driveway. "Security guard. Frederick-Fish-face."

"Let's follow him," Poet said.

"Like spies," Meeka said.

"Yeah," Poet said. "I've always wondered if security guards pick their noses while they're out security-ing by themselves."

"Or fart really loudly."

"Or burp in time to music," Poet said. "We should make sure he doesn't go near Miss Cowan's house while the boys are there."

"Mind you, they'd hear him if he farted and burped in time to music all at once," Meeka said. "He'd be a burfarty expert."

Poet gave her a hug. "Welcome back, Meeka. I missed you."

Logan sneaked around the back, Nate close behind.

An open window! Fantastic. But less fantastic when Nate pushed him through too fast and his foot landed in the toilet bowl.

"If you had to go, you just needed to say," Nate said when he got inside and saw Logan wringing out his sock.

Logan flicked him in the face with it.

"I thought women always put the lid down." He took his other shoe off and left it by the bath. "Don't let me forget my shoes."

They tiptoed around the house. It was full of colourful rugs and bright cushions and show-stopping art on the wall. One wall was covered in drawings by kids. Love hearts, doctors, syringes, monkeys, angels, bedpans, and an ugly hunchback man, eating cake. And someone with big blue eyes, green lips, and green hair smiling over everybody.

"This is weird," Nate said.

"I expected ... Well, I don't know what I expected. Something dark and dreary. Not all this colour," Logan said.

"I know. It's like walking into a rainbow," Nate said.

"That's something Poet would say," Logan said.

"Do you think I could get Poet to come to parkour with me? She was great at climbing that tree. Mum might say yes if two of us wanted to do it."

"Don't think so. She's only into climbing because she's into Jungle Wars. It won't last. She'd rather lie on her bed watching YouTube," Logan said. "Look at this." He pointed to the wallpaper image on the computer he'd turned on.

"Is that who I think it is?" Nate asked.

"Yep. It's Brody Bankston, some bald guy, and the blue-eyed, green-haired pixie from those kid's pictures on the wall."

"How does Miss Cowan know Brody Bankston? And who are those other two people?"

"Now that's a mystery," Logan said. "Friends?"

"Do you think Miss Cowan has friends? Especially Brody Bankston?"

"Stranger things have happened. What do you think her password is?"

"Try 'Brody'," Nate said.

Nope.

"Jungle Wars."

Nope.

"Cowan123"

Nope.

"I've got an idea," Logan said. He typed in, 'IHATEMATHS'.

Cracked it!

"How did you know?" Nate asked.

"A feeling I've had about Miss Cowan. I think she's the opposite of everything she seems to be. But what I can't work out is if that's good or bad," Logan said.

"Well, you do notice stuff, sometimes. Totally missed Meeka's jealousy but we can move past that and still trust your instincts," Nate said.

"Thanks, Ninja." Logan went to the browser and looked up History.

"Look at this. Heaps of maths sites."

"Why would an expert in maths need to look at all those sites?" Nate asked.

"Maybe she isn't an expert after all," Logan said. "Look at this. This is interesting."

It was a security company website. They clicked through.

"It's the spec page for a safe," Nate said.

"You know, Jason pointed one out to me the other day when he showed me around. They have that safe here. And look, here's a YouTube video showing how to break into it."

"She's going to steal stuff from their safe. She's a thief!"

They heard a noise outside. A light beamed through the window.

"Get down," Logan said.

They both ducked.

"Hi, Frederick," Logan heard Meeka call.

The light moved away.

"Miss Castaneda-Whitley. Shouldn't you be watching your movie?" a male voice said. Frederick?

"We're on the way there now. Everything okay with you?"

"Fine. Thought I heard movement in Miss Cowan's place, that's all," he said. The light shone back in again. Nate clutched his arm.

"She's out. We saw her go. She said if we saw you to tell you not to worry about her place tonight. She's been having trouble with rats and has left a few traps out. Hoping to catch a big one."

"Maybe that's what you heard—a trap going off!" Poet said.

"We should go see," Meeka said.

"I dunno, Meeka, Miss Cowan said she'd put five or six traps out and if anyone went in there, they'd probably end up with one on their foot."

"Ohhh." Meeka sounded sad.

"We better leave it," the security guard said. "And you kids better start watching your movie. It's supposed to be two hours long. How there can be that much going on in a jungle is beside me."

"You don't like movies, Frederick?" Poet asked.

"Not much," the security guard said, his voice fading with his departing footsteps.

"Phew," Nate said. "Hope we don't stand on any rat traps. Especially you, with your bare feet."

"Very funny. That was quick thinking from Meeka."

The heavy footsteps changed direction. The guard was coming back.

"You girls keep going. I'm going to check around the back," he called.

"He'll see the open window!" Nate whispered.

"What about my shoes?" He needed to get his shoes!

"I can hear him coming around the back," Nate said. "We've got to go out the front right now."

What about his shoes? What would Miss Cowan think when she saw them? He'd have to get them back before she came home.

Chapter Eleven:
Escaping Jungle Wars

Saturday 8.30pm

Logan was impressed with the home theatre. "How many people can this place seat?"

"About sixty." Meeka didn't look at him. Was she embarrassed or still being rude?

"I've got to go back and get my shoes," Logan said. "I left them in Miss Cowan's bathroom."

"You'll have to wait until Frederick-Fish-Face has moved on. He'll be round the other side of this house in half an hour. He's like clockwork," Meeka said.

"And you know that because?" Nate asked.

"Because sometimes I need to not be seen," Meeka said. "There's always someone watching me."

The door opened and in walked Gillian.

"See?" Meeka said.

"Oh good, you haven't started yet," Gillian said. "Been raiding the kitchen, have you?"

"No, not that," Meeka said. "We had a hard time getting the boys away from the Xbox."

Was lying her second language? She did it without even thinking.

"Well, for once I'm glad for Xbox. I'd love to watch the movie with you guys, if you don't mind." Gillian smiled and her whole faced glowed.

She was a piece of work. That was something his father used to say. Logan had never understood what the phrase meant, but he was beginning to figure it out.

"I brought some snacks, in case you'd forgotten," Gillian said. She pulled out some potato crisps and other treats from her bag.

"Well, I am kind of hungry," Nate said. "Let's get the movie started."

What was Nate thinking? How could he encourage her to stay? How was Logan going to get away now?

Gillian and Meeka set up the movie while Poet hovered near them. Maybe she didn't trust Gillian either.

Nate came and sat beside him with a bag of popcorn.

"What are you doing?" Logan whispered. "Has she cast you under her spell as well?"

"I knew you didn't trust her. Me neither," Nate whispered back. "You should eat some of this popcorn. It's got pistachios in it."

"So?" Logan whispered. How could Nate be so frustrating?

"Don't pistachios give you a sore tummy? Make you have to sit on the toilet for, I dunno, at least thirty minutes? Maybe even an hour?"

Logan smiled. He could've hugged Nate. Gross.

"Better wait half an hour so she's really hooked into Brody without his shirt on," Nate said.

"What if he keeps it on for longer than half an hour? I've got to get back to Miss Cowan's before she gets home again."

"Didn't you see the trailer for this movie?" Nate said. "I don't think he even owns a shirt. But he's got some cool guns."

"You don't mind guns even after you've had one pointed at your head?"

Nate sat very still, and then shivered.

"That was real. This is make-believe. It's totally different. But thanks for spoiling the only good part about the movie for me."

"Sorry," Logan whispered.

"It's okay. I'll probably get into it anyway," Nate said. "I'm mindless like that."

"Are you guys ready?" Gillian looked at Poet. "They're not going to talk all the way through the movie, are they?"

"Only during the romantic parts," Poet said. "And they yell a lot during the action scenes."

"So pretty much the whole way through then," Gillian said.

The movie wasn't bad. Might even be better than Jungle Wars One. Logan checked the time on his phone. Time to go. Well, time to leave—he wasn't really going to 'go'. He moaned.

"It's not a romantic part yet, Logan," Gillian said.

He moaned a bit louder and stood up. "Were there pistachios in that popcorn?" he asked in between groans.

"Oh, no. Sorry, Logan!" Nate said.

Loud. Way too loud. Tone it down, Nate.

"I better go," Logan said.

"Pistachios. They give him the bellyache. He'll probably be on the loo for an hour," Nate said.

Meeka frowned. Was she going to say something?

Poet's leg moved. Must've stood on Meeka's foot.

Thank you, Poet! Thank goodness she was used to Nate. Anything he said, she played along with.

"I'm so sorry," Gillian said. "I had no idea. Your parents didn't tell me when I asked about allergies."

"It's not really an allergy," Poet said. "If he was allergic, he'd be blown up as big as a whale right now." She puffed out her cheeks and rocked in her chair with her arms outstretched.

"It's that thing... that thing... Food intolerance." Nate said. "He's okay if he eats a little bit, but then if he eats too much..." He took a breath and shook his head.

Logan groaned.

"You better go, scooterfeet," Nate said.

"We can watch the rest of the movie tomorrow," Gillian said.

"Nooo." Logan groaned. "I don't even like it. You keep watching it. I gotta... gotta go." He headed towards the door, still groaning.

"Can we please keep watching, Gillian?" Poet pulled on Gillian's arm.

"I guess so," Gillian cleared her throat. "Shouldn't we do something for you, Logan?"

Logan shook his head and groaned.

"He'll be okay. Give him an hour and he'll be back to normal," Nate said. "Can we please keep watching? I think there's going to be some cool stunts soon."

"Please." Poet gave a great impression of a street beggar.

Gillian took a deep breath. "Okay then. I'll check on you in awhile, Logan."

"You don't want to do that," Nate said, pinching his nose.

Gillian looked at him and frowned. "Let's get back to the movie then."

Logan made his escape. Hopefully Miss Cowan was still out.

Chapter Twelve:
Miss Cowan Mystery

Saturday 9.15pm

Logan ran to Miss Cowan's house. The sun had dropped over the horizon, and there were no lights on inside. She still wasn't home. Great!

He ducked around the back, but the window was shut. Thanks a lot, Fred. Maybe he'd pushed it shut and it wasn't latched. He crept over to the window.

"Missing something?" a voice called out from above.

Above?

He looked up. Someone was peering over the edge of the roof.

"Miss Cowan?" he asked.

No way! On the roof? How'd she even get there?

"I need to talk to you. There's a tree around the side you can climb. It's got a branch that hangs over the roof. You can jump down onto it."

Whaaat?

"Hurry up, please." That was definitely Miss Cowan's voice.

He headed to the side of the house.

"Other side, please," Miss Cowan called out.

Sure enough, there was a tree. Not the easiest tree to climb. If Miss Cowan could do this and he couldn't, maybe he did have scooterfeet. That wasn't a pleasant thought.

The jump down to the roof wasn't easy either.

"You can do it, Logan. It's not that far." Her tone was kind. This was getting way too weird.

"I'm not going to hurt you." Still the kind voice. Maybe Miss Cowan had been taken over by aliens.

"You're not a zombie, are you?" Logan called out.

"Not today. But if we don't figure out what to do about Gillian, we'll probably all wish we were zombies." Kind voice again. "Come on, get down here." Back to mean Miss Cowan teacher voice. That was much better.

He jumped down.

"Bet that hurt without your shoes on," Miss Cowan said. And grinned.

Grinned!

She handed him his shoes. "Cold feet?"

"Yep," Logan said, not taking his eyes off her.

"Got you some dry socks. They're my brother's, so you don't have to worry about wearing girl's socks and all that. They may be a bit big, that's all." She handed him a pair of plain black socks.

"Who ARE you?" Logan asked.

Miss Cowan smiled. "You said that just like in the movies. 'Who ARE you?' I always wanted someone to say that to me. Had hoped I'd be more a spy character than a nasty old school teacher."

She sat down and pointed to the spot beside her on her left.

"Sit," she said. Back to mean old school teacher voice.

He sat.

"Your wart's on the wrong side."

"What?" she said and punched out a breath. "I hate that wart."

"Please tell me who you are. I'm getting scared," Logan said.

"No, you're only curious. Which is why you broke into my house."

Half kind, half mean teacher.

"Did you figure anything out?" she asked.

"You left in a hurry, you're hopeless at maths, have a crush on Brody Bankston, don't know how to mix and match colours for what Poet would call 'a harmonious effect', and are planning on stealing stuff from Meeka's parents safe."

"Left in a hurry?"

"Toilet seat was up," he said and waved his foot around.

She laughed. She had a nice laugh.

"Sorry about that," she said. "I'm usually good with colours. Been stressed lately, which makes everything else kind of crazy. You're off with stealing stuff from Meeka's parents. I'm actually planning on stealing stuff from Gillian."

"You're a thief!" Logan said.

"Nope, wrong again. I don't usually have much to do with thieves, being a teacher and all that. But I used to know a few, which is going to be helpful when I get into Gillian's house. One of them has texted me exactly what I need to do to open her safe."

"What do you want to get from Gillian's safe?"

"You're good, Logan. Very good. I like how you keep asking questions. You'd be a good detective. You're not shocked by the fact I want to steal something from lovely-dovely Gillian." Her voice sounded sour.

"Gillian is up to something. I don't know what. And I don't know what you're up to. But I'd really like to. Especially if it's going to hurt Meeka," Logan tried to sound fierce.

Miss Cowan smiled at him and patted his hand.

Obviously he'd frightened her.

"You're great, Logan. We could've stopped all this nonsense ages ago if you'd been here sooner. Meeka is hiding something. I know what it is, but I only found out last night. She really likes you and Nate and Poet, so it's up to her to tell you when she's ready. Gillian knows her secret and is blackmailing her into going along with all this horrible school stuff because Meeka's too scared to tell her parents about it."

"Horrible school stuff? Why are you teaching her if you don't like it?"

"Because I'm trying to help Meeka."

"By making her do work she hates. Even on a Saturday? She hates you, you know."

Miss Cowan sighed.

"I know. Breaks my heart, but if I don't teach what Gillian wants, she'll fire me. And if Meeka likes me, Gillian will fire me. Have you not noticed that all Meeka's friends have been fired?"

"Violet resigned," Logan said.

"No. Gillian lied about that. She was fired," Miss Cowan said. "I'm the only one standing between Meeka and Gillian. I've heard Meeka call her a witch, and that's what she is. Gillian the witch. She has everyone else wrapped around her fingers. No one's asking any questions at all. Meeka will be at boarding school within a month if we don't do something."

"But why? Why would Gillian do all that?" Logan asked.

"I think it's something to do with all the robberies going on in the neighbourhood," Miss Cowan said.

Logan thought for a minute. Okay, he'd say it.

"What about the skimmer? What were you doing with that?"

"Credit card skimmer?" She tipped her head to the side and touched her throat.

He nodded.

"I don't have anything to do with credit card fraud," she said, frowning. "Why would you think I did?"

"A courier dropped off a parcel for you the other night. It was a vacuum cleaner and inside it was a credit card skimmer."

"How do you even know what that is?" she asked.

"It came with an instruction sheet," he said.

"Like 'Five easy steps to using your credit card skimmer for health and wealth'?"

"Uh-huh."

"Bizarre. What's the world coming to?"

"You don't look so scary without your glasses."

"Thank you. How come I never saw this package? It must've been big."

"It was left outside Andrew's door. We went to take it inside, but it fell open and we saw the skimmer."

"Then what did you do with it?" she asked.

"Gillian found us and took it off us. Said she was going to investigate and we shouldn't tell anyone. She was going to give it back to you."

"Well, she never did. Why would the courier deliver it to Andrew? My house comes first and is easy to find. Andrew is never home, fool that he is." She was talking to herself. She suddenly looked at him, her eyes gleaming.

"That's it. The skimmer was for Gillian. She's running some kind of crime operation from here. It's the perfect place. Jason and Lia are often away. Andrew's smitten with her. If she can get Andrew to go off with Jason more often, then all she needs to do is ship Meeka off to boarding school and she has the run of the place."

Miss Cowan might be onto something.

"Did she employ the new security guard?" Logan asked.

"Yep. Frederick-Fish-Face. And the cook. And the gardener. And the cleaners." She tapped him on the shoulder with each person she said. "Stupid me. I thought she wanted to get rid of Meeka so she could marry Andrew and have all his attention to herself. This is much better."

"I think it's much worse," Logan said. "You're trying to tell me there's some kind of crime ring running out of Meeka's home."

"Yep." Her face dropped."But what can we do about it? Nobody will talk to me, let alone believe me. Gillian set me up to be a prime suspect with the credit card skimmer. I'm running out of options. I don't even know where she is right now. If she was out tonight, it would be perfect."

"She's watching Jungle Wars Two with Meeka and the others. There's still at least an hour to go."

"I should've known. Do all females love watching Brody with his shirt off?" She shook her head.

"How do you know Brody Bankston?" Logan asked.

"You wouldn't believe me if I told you. Another time, maybe. I've got to go now."

"Wait. Why do you even care? You've only known Meeka a short time," Logan said.

"I've known her for ages. It's a long story." Miss Cowan looked sad. "Right now, I've got to go and do something about Gillian blackmailing her. You can't let Meeka know you've talked to me. If she thinks I'm not Miss Cowan, she'll give me away to Gillian. She'll be so excited, and then Gillian will do something desperate. She's dangerous, Logan."

She moved her wart to her other side and pulled her glasses over her eyes.

"Logan. Did you hear me? I said she's dangerous." Horrible Mean Teacher Voice.

"So, what do we do next?" Logan asked.

"You do nothing. You can't let Meeka know about me, and you can't let her know that you know she's being blackmailed. I'm going to go to the police tomorrow morning. I know someone who can help, keep it quiet to protect Lia and Jason's reputations. You go back to the others. Whatever happens, don't leave Meeka alone with Gillian. She bruised Meeka's shoulders the other day, and I'm sure she's slapped her in the face as well."

Logan jumped up. "No way!"

"I'm not kidding. I wish I were. That's why I always try to stop Meeka being alone with Gillian. I've got to sort this out now, before I get fired or there will be no one here to keep her safe. I need you to keep an eye on Meeka. Just for one more day, then you can go tell Jason everything. Not that he'll believe anything I've told you. But he may be able to convince Meeka to tell the truth. She adores him."

Meeka being hit? That couldn't go on. He had to do something about it now.

Miss Cowan stood up.

"Make sure Meeka's not alone. Then Gillian can't hurt her. It's only until lunchtime tomorrow, not even a whole day. Then I'll be back with the police to sort out Gillian. Can you keep it a secret until then? Please? Otherwise Gillian will leave and find someone else to hurt."

"How do I know you're telling the truth and it's not you who's hurting Meeka?" he asked, his voice shaking.

She closed her eyes for half a minute. Then she pulled out her phone and opened a photo app.

"This is Meeka when she was six, learning to skateboard. We took the skateboard off her when she attached it to Violet's tow bar with a rope and rode along behind her down the street. Violet almost had a heart attack when she saw her in the rear-view mirror."

She flicked to another picture.

"This is Meeka when she was seven, after Walter caught her about to jump off the veranda into the swimming pool, like in the movies. She'd have never made it. Walter told Jason about it and he turned it into an inside pool."

She flicked through more pictures.

"This is Meeka at the fairground when she was eight and sneaked onto the rollercoaster she was too small to ride. Freaked us all out. When she was nine she wanted to build a tree hut, so Walter and I put a platform up for her in that other tree. It had some netting for sides then, but she figured out how to get rid of them before her Dad came home so he wouldn't notice it. Oh, here's a nice one. This is Meeka when she was nine and trying to teach Violet how to use a computer."

She smiled and shook her head. "Violet's really good at making Meeka's favourite marshmallow men meringues, but she's never going to figure out a computer. Here's Meeka at an explosives science course when she was ten. She was trying to mix chemicals in the garden shed so she could make explosives like her dad. Walter and I took her to the science course, then to the hospital to meet some burn victims. She gave up on that idea after that."

"She's quite dangerous, isn't she?" Logan said.

"But wait, there's more," Miss Cowan said. "This is Meeka just before she met you guys. Walter caught her trying to break into Andrew's gun cabinet. She wanted to take a gun to pieces, like they do in the movies. Thought it would impress her dad. We took her to the gun range and gave her a lesson in gun safety and told her some scary stories. Then we taught her how to pull a gun to pieces and put it back together. It's not that hard, and she's quite fast. She never told her dad though. She worked out he might not like that one."

"Lia would have fit," Logan said.

"Oh, yeah!" Miss Cowan grinned.

It was unsettling, seeing her smile like that.

"How come you're not in any of the photos?" he asked.

"I took the photos. And you wouldn't recognise me if I was in them. I look nothing like I do now." She grimaced. "I look more like an elf. I don't fit in with all these glamorous people. I'm kind of glad to dress like this so I don't have to try and be beautiful."

She looked sad. Like she wanted to be beautiful.

"I like elves," he said.

"Yes, but no one takes them seriously. But you will listen to me, won't you? You'll keep the whole Meeka thing a secret until lunchtime tomorrow?"

"All right, but I only believe you because Meeka's told me before her most favourite food is Violet's marshmallow men meringues. What does she call them?"

"Merangalow Men, of course," she said. "You get down off the roof by shimmying down the drain pipe."

She crouched down and slid over the edge of the roof.

"I got it!" Logan shouted.

"Shhh, keep it down!"

He crouched down and leaned out over the wall. "You're her guardian pixie," he said just loud enough for her to hear.

"I wish she wouldn't call me that. Can't I be an angel once in my life?"

Logan watched her leave. Was he going to leave her to break into Gillian's house by herself? She might need some backup. Especially if she was a pixie.

He jumped down and went after her.

Chapter Thirteen:
Breaking into Gillian's House

Saturday night, 9.45pm

Meeka sat in the dark, not watching the movie at all.

What was going on? Where had Logan gone? He wasn't allergic or intolerant to nuts. Especially pistachios. The day he'd met her he'd eaten three whole packets before firing half a packet in Mum's hair.

The thought made her smile.

Logan was a good friend. He'd saved her life! How could she be so mean to him? It wasn't his problem Dad ignored her.

She slumped in her seat.

Okay, he hadn't exactly ignored her. The truth was her wonderful father was hardly ever there for her any more. Maybe he wasn't so perfect after all. Maybe he had faults. Great big horrible faults. Grigblefaults.

She sighed. A big long sigh.

Gillian looked at her.

Meeka sat up and smiled.

Don't let her talk to me. Please, no.

Brody came back on screen. Gillian turned back to watch him.

That Brody reminded Meeka of someone. What was she just thinking?

Oh, her Dad. He was her hero. How could she think anything bad about him? Was this part of growing up? It sucked. She wanted that wonderful glowing sunshiny feeling when she thought of him, like normal. But even if she closed her eyes hard and pictured him, all she got was an ache. A bellyache.

She opened her eyes.

She should go check on Logan and his sore tummy. Better than sitting here thinking how Dad let her down. Especially with Gillian. Did he even care?

Something wet trickled down her face.

Cut that out!

She sniffed and stood up.

"I'm going to go check on Logan. You guys keep watching. I'll see it with Dad another time."

Not likely. He'd probably have to leave before he had any time to spend with her. Making movies was more important than her. Best to spend her time on people who'd give back. People like Logan and Nate and Poet. Gillian couldn't fire them.

"You look a bit upset, Meeka. Are you all right?" Gillian asked.

Like she cared. Witch.

"I'm good. Worried about Logan, that's all. We had a bit of a fight. I need to go apologise. You guys keep watching. It's Brody Bankston, after all." She tried to smile. Could this get any worse? *Come on, Nate. Come on, Poet. Do your thing!*

"Your dad will be disappointed if you don't see it," Gillian said. "He had to argue hard with your Mum and Abby to let you girls watch it. It's rated 12a. I'm sure Logan will come back when he's ready."

Meeka was going to lose it if someone didn't do something soon.

"Oh, I hadn't thought about that," Nate said. "Did Mum ask you to stay with the girls? Because of the scary parts?"

"What?" Gillian asked.

"That's so nice of you, Gillian." Poet stood up. "If it's a scary movie, I usually sit by Mum and hold her hand and she covers my eyes in the scary parts. Could I sit by you and hold your hand? Some of the movie has been pretty scary."

She sat down by Gillian and grabbed her hand. Gillian stared at her.

"Poet, I'll sit on your other side, and cover your eyes in the scary parts." Nate stood and thumbed for Meeka to leave.

"Are you sure, Meeka? We can finish watching this later," Gillian called out to her.

"It's all good, Gillian." She had to stop herself from running out the door.

"Can you take the movie back a bit, Gillian?" she heard Nate ask. "We've missed an action scene."

"And Brody looked particularly fine," Poet said.

Meeka stepped out of the room.

Particularly fine, my foot. Andrew and Dad had more muscles than him. And since when did she care about guy's muscles? She must be growing up.

That was scary.

She spotted Logan sneaking away from Miss Cowan's. She checked the time on her phone. Fish-face would be the other side of Andrew's now, out of the way. She phoned Logan.

"What are you doing?" came his voice in her ear. "Someone else will hear the phone ring!"

"It shouldn't have rung loud. Didn't you put it on vibrate for the movie? How thoughtless," she said. "What you up to, sneaking around like that?"

"I'm not talking to you," Logan said.

"Then why did you answer the phone?" Meeka asked.

She was beginning to enjoy this.

Silence.

"Logan?" she asked.

"That's me not talking to you," he said.

"I wouldn't talk to me either if I were you. Sorry for being a jerk up the tree," she said.

"Guess you had a tree-jerk reaction."

"That's so lame."

"Sorry. And sorry for stealing your dad. You can have him back. Two fathers are more than enough. Even if one of them is in prison."

"Thanks, Logan. I haven't decided if I want him back. He's been a jerk too lately. Maximo Jerkio."

"Parents suck sometimes. But you have a good one. Take it from me. I'm the king of bad dads."

"I guess he can be okay, but I'd never realised he can be so wrong. Not until now, that is."

"Everyone makes mistakes," Logan said. "Except for Nate."

"Except for Nate." Meeka said at the same time.

Logan appeared in front of her. They hung up their phones.

"Friends?" Logan asked and put his hands on her shoulders.

"Friends," Meeka said.

Logan squeezed her shoulders. Meeka took a quick breath in. That really hurt. But she couldn't let Logan know. He'd be wound-up-tight upset.

"What were you doing, sneaking around?" Meeka asked.

Logan sighed.

"I was going to break into Gillian's house. There's something about her I don't like."

There was a lot about Gillian that Meeka didn't like. But it might not be safe for Logan to break in there. And what if he found out what Meeka had done? She needed to keep an eye on him.

"How'd it go at Miss Cowan's? Did you find anything?"

"Nothing but maths books. If she's a criminal, she's hiding it well," he said.

"That's disappointing. But it's a bit risky breaking into Gillian's. Fish-face will be around soon."

"Oh no," Logan said, wincing. "I better go."

He looked worried.

"I'm coming too," Meeka said.

"I think it'd be better if I went by myself. Less likely to get caught and all that." He walked away.

What was going on? She ran after him.

"I'll show you how to get in the back window," she said.

He stopped and looked at her, his teeth gritted. He didn't want her to come.

She pouted.

He ran his hand though his hair and started walking again.

"As long as the toilet lid's down," he said.

"Huh?"

"Nothing."

Logan's neck muscles were so tense he could have used his head as a hammer. How could he make sure Meeka didn't see Miss Cowan at Gillian's?

And she did have sore shoulders. Why wouldn't she tell anyone?

"Over here, Logan." Meeka was pointing to an open window.

He climbed in. Slowly. The toilet lid was down.

Of course. It was Gillian. Everything in place.

He jumped down.

Banged on the lid.

He stepped off and pretended to fall over, knocking the toothbrush container on the floor.

That made a loud noise too.

"What are you doing Logan?" Meeka hissed.

He picked up the toothbrush container and slammed it onto the vanity.

Then he had a coughing fit.

"Have you lost your mind? We're trying to sneak. You know, quietly." Meeka crawled in the window behind him.

"Oh, sorry," he said in a loud voice.

Meeka's mouth dropped wide open.

"Sorry," he whispered.

Oh God, this isn't as desperate as when you saved us from that fire, but please don't let Miss Cowan be here.

What was he doing? Praying? It might help. It worked last time.

It's up to you now, God.

He stepped out into the hallway and made his way to the lounge. The lamp on the piano was turned on. He stepped into the kitchen. The back door was open. He glimpsed Miss Cowan wave at him before she disappeared behind a tree.

Miss Cowan in jeans and sneakers. He hadn't noticed that before. That was mind-maulingly weird.

He turned back to Meeka.

"Someone's been here before us," he said.

"Oh no." Meeka ran back down the hallway to the office.

He followed her. She was staring at the open safe in the wall.

"It's not there. It's not there." She was rocking herself.

"What's not there?" Logan asked.

If only he could shake her, but her shoulders were too sore. He's hardly touched her before and she'd almost jumped out of her skin. He knew what that felt like. Best not to touch her.

"What's not there, Meeka?" he asked again, louder this time.

Meeka stopped rocking and stared at him.

"Come on, Meeka. You can tell me. What's going on?" he asked.

"I can't! I can't tell you anything. I wish you'd never come!" She ran through the door, down the hall, and out the kitchen door.

Logan wanted to beat his head against the nearest wall.

His phone beeped.

Stupid phone. He should've put it on vibrate.

Text message from Nate.

You need to get back. Movie is finishing soon. Can't hold Gillian here much longer.

Oh, no. He'd forgotten about Gillian.

He looked around. Miss Cowan probably wouldn't want anyone to know she'd been there. He shut the safe, turned off the light, and crept out the kitchen door, locking it behind him.

He made his way back to the house, went past Meeka's room and knocked on her door.

"Meeka, it's me. Logan. Can we talk?"

The door opened. Only a crack.

"Sorry about before, Logan. I'll tell you all about it tomorrow. I need to sleep now. Please tell Mum and Dad I've gone to bed if you see them."

"Promise you'll talk to me," he said. "Remember the night we met, and we sat by the bonfire? You said you'd never lie to me."

She sniffed.

"I know," she whispered. "You're the one friend I can trust. I should've told you guys a long time ago. But I was younger then. I thought Dad would rescue me. I'll tell you tomorrow. I want to sleep on it now."

"Okay. Promise me you'll tell me. Promise."

"I promise," she said.

The door shut. Logan leaned his head against it. He was tired. So tired.

Meeka was in a lot of trouble. If only she'd let him help. He was going to have to tell Jason if she wouldn't. Then she'd never talk to him again. At all.

But there was no way he'd let someone keep hurting her. His phone vibrated. Nate.

Where are you?

Time to go tell a few more lies. He headed back down the hall. He couldn't wait until lunchtime tomorrow. When Miss Cowan would be back with the police.

He stopped.

As long as Miss Cowan wasn't lying to him.

What if all she wanted was what was in the safe? What if she was Meeka's enemy and not her friend?

What if Miss Cowan was the one hurting Meeka?

Chapter Fourteen:
Waiting For His Turn

Sunday Morning, 8.30am

Logan glanced up as Lia walked into the dining room the next morning.

"Gillian's house was burgled last night," she said.

"No way!" Abby said.

"Are you alright Logan?" Lia asked. "You look pale. Jason is looking over the house with Gillian and a policeman she knows. Looks like only her jewellery from the safe was taken. The policeman's going to want to talk to you kids, but it's no big deal. Don't look so worried Logan."

He was worried. What if the policeman found out he'd broken into Gillian's? Was he a thief? Like his father?

Lia patted his arm then looked at Abby and Steve. "No one can find Miss Cowan."

They couldn't find Miss Cowan because she had left for the police already. Surely that was the only reason.

"I saw her go out last night in her car," Poet said. "Before the movie."

"Yes, but the security guard saw her come back before the movie ended," Lia said. "And her car is still here."

How could she go to the police without her car?

"Maybe she's gone for a run?" Logan said. She ran fast last night, when she left Gillian's.

"Miss Cowan?" Andrew snorted. "She wouldn't know how to run. Unless she's doing a runner."

All the adults nodded.

"I hope she's okay and not hurt," Poet said. "You know, the burglar could've beaten her up or something if she got in the way."

"I hadn't thought of that," Abby said. "Even I'm thinking the worst of her just because she's a bit grouchy."

Jason walked in slowly. His smile faded almost as soon as it hit his mouth.

"Where's Meeka?" he asked.

"She didn't want to come down for breakfast," Lia said. "Wants to talk to you later about spending some time together today. How'd it go with the police?"

"All right, I guess. He didn't seem very thorough. Not like the police after those smugglers caught you lot. But I guess it's not so serious."

His phone rang. "I have to take this. Sorry." He walked out the room, talking into the phone. "Wasn't expecting you for another month."

The kids ate their breakfast in silence while the adults and Cole talked about the show they'd seen.

"I sketched some of the costumes," Cole said. He picked up his sketch pad from the seat beside him. "Someone's written on my drawing!"

"What?" Abby asked.

"Look at this." He held the open sketch pad out to Abby.

"Great work, but if you use some more irregular lines when shading it will add a lot of dynamism to your sketch." She looked up at Cole. "Sounds like good advice. Who would write that?"

"Miss Cowan maybe. Sounds like teacher-talk," Nate said.

"Miss Cowan can't draw," Andrew said. "I saw her try once. She was hopeless."

Andrew sure was negative about Miss Cowan. She didn't deserve that.

"Can you think of anything good Miss Cowan can do?" Logan asked.

"Leave," Andrew said.

Logan, Nate, and Poet stared at him.

"What?" he said. "It's how I feel. Sorry."

"You know, I think once that policeman finishes today, we should all go into the city together," Steve said. "I'm sure Jason or Andrew will lend us a car and we could have some family time."

"You don't need to go," Andrew said. "Sorry for being so negative. I'm worried about Meeka. She hasn't come out of her room today. It's not like her."

"It might not be her teacher's fault," Logan said.

Now everyone stared at him.

"Logan, you'd tell us if there was something going on with Meeka, wouldn't you?" Lia asked.

"Of course," Logan said.

"I think she wants to spend some time with her dad," Poet said.

"Yes, that's all it is," Nate said.

"And spend time with me she shall," Jason said, coming back in the room. "Cheer up, everyone. I have a surprise for you all! I have to take Meeka to collect it. Andrew, if you come, Meeka and I can chat in the back on the way. Kill two birds with one stone."

"How long will it take?" Andrew asked.

"A bit over an hour," Jason said.

Good one Jason. That's quality one-on-one time. She'll really open up to you with grumpy Andrew in the front.

"I'll go get Meeka and meet you in the car," Jason said to Andrew. "It'll be great, guys. Trust me." He smiled the smile that sent stunt people through the front window and onto the bonnet of speeding cars. Somehow it didn't seem to glow so much this morning.

Logan only had to wait until lunchtime. There was still plenty of time for Miss Cowan to get back with her police friends. If she was for real, that was. Where was she?

Logan and the others sat around in the lounge, waiting.

Nate and Poet talked to the policeman, one at a time.

Poet finished and came back to the lounge. Logan was next. He wrung his hands.

Gillian appeared at the door.

"The police officer has to go back to the station," she said. "I'm going to go with him to give my statement, then I'll get some lunch. Logan, I'll collect you and Meeka and take you to the station at about one o'clock to give your statements."

"Can't they do it here?" Steve asked.

"He's run out of time—he has a few things to deal with there. I can work around him to give the rest of my statement and then he'll have some more time about one o'clock. I'm happy to take Logan and Meeka. I'll bring them right back, so they won't miss out on too much of the surprise."

"I guess that'll be okay. I'll come too." Steve squeezed Logan's shoulder.

Thank goodness for Steve. But what would he say if he found out Logan had broken into Gillian's? He'd be so mad. And disappointed. Logan's shoulders sagged.

"It's not necessary. But as you wish." Gillian frowned and turned to leave.

"Oh," she said, turning back. "I saw Miss Cowan. Very strange. She walked in on me and my police friend, took one look at him, mumbled something and walked out again. I think she's hiding something."

"Did you see where she went?" Cole asked.

"No. She'd disappeared by the time the officer got outside. He said not to worry, that he'd track her down. Anyhow, there he is now. I better go."

Logan walked to the door with Steve and watched them drive off. "Funny that he didn't stay and finish the job. Or go after Miss Cowan," Steve said, his arm around Logan.

Maybe Logan should talk to Steve now.

Andrew drove up.

"Well, we better go see what the surprise is," Steve said. "Come on, everyone."

Logan felt so tense. The last thing he needed now was a surprise. Where was Miss Cowan?

As they stepped outside, Miss Cowan appeared from the direction of Gillian's house.

Logan breathed a sigh of relief. She hadn't run off.

She walked straight up to Jason as he hopped out of the car.

"There you are Miss Cowan," he said. "We were worried about you."

"Don't lie," she said. "You're no good at it. I need to talk to you now. In private. It's urgent." She grabbed his arm.

Chapter Fifteen:
The Truth About Miss Cowan

Logan watched Jason's face turn to stone.

Jason was lying. He hadn't been worried about Miss Cowan. But he was Jason Whitley. What was wrong with Miss Cowan? Nobody would ever call him a liar.

"I think not, Miss Cowan," Jason said. "You'll be able to talk to the police officer when he gets back. I saw him drive off, but I expect we'll see him again. Right now I have something to take everyone's mind off the burglary last night."

Andrew got out of the car and stood by Jason.

"Is that your answer to everything?" Miss Cowan's voice started to rise. "You've just been burgled, but let's have a party! Don't you take anything seriously?" Her eyes bulged behind her glasses.

"That's enough, Miss Cowan." Andrew held her arm.

She yanked her arm back, grabbed Andrew's wrist with her other hand, and twisted it. He went down on one knee. She was fast. And she made it look easy. How did she know how to do that?

Miss Cowan took a deep breath. "You have no right to talk to anyone, Andrew. You haven't been taking your job seriously for the last month."

"You're way out of line Miss Cowan," Jason said. "I suggest you stop right there."

"Stop?" she said. "Stop? You have no idea how much danger Meeka and the kids are in. You only want to pretend that everything is always fine. Well, it's not! You didn't just see the Fireman sitting talking to that witch, Gillian. They've gone now, but they'll be back."

"Gillian is not a witch! And what do you mean, a fireman?" Andrew stood up and waved his arm towards the driveway. "He was a policeman."

"What do you know? You've hardly been here the last month. And it's the same every year. You go away or try to make yourself busy so you don't have to grieve the death of your wife and daughter. I am so sick of it — it's been thirteen years, for crying out loud!"

Andrew took a step back, shaking as if he'd been punched.

Miss Cowan's hand flew to her mouth. "Oh, Andrew. I'm so sorry. I didn't mean that. I'm just so upset.

She sobbed. "If only Brody were here, none of this would have happened."

Someone coughed from behind the car. "I am here, Tessa. What on earth are you doing?"

Was that Brody Bankston? Unbelievable! This was like a scene from a movie. Maybe there were cameras somewhere.

"Brody." Miss Cowan started to sway.

Brody Bankston slid over the bonnet and ran to her.

"You're here." She collapsed, but he managed to catch her as she fell. He turned to face them all, holding Miss Cowan in his arms.

It must be a movie! Logan looked around for cameras, but there weren't any. He looked back at Brody. It really was Brody Bankston. And he was holding Miss Cowan! Impossible!

"Hi everyone," he said. "I'm Brody Bankston. And this, this is my sister. My twin sister." He looked at her and grimaced. "Well, she sounds like my sister. I wouldn't have known by looking at her." He shook his head. "Oh Tessa, have you got some explaining to do."

"What!" Jason shouted. "Miss Cowan is your twin? No way. She's nothing like you!"

"I can see you're a bit upset, Jason." Brody nodded.

"Upset! Did you hear any of what she said? What she said to Andrew?"

"Yes, yes. I got most of it—she was kind of loud. Did she say the Fireman was sitting talking to a witch?"

"That's right," Logan said. "The witch is Gillian. Who's the Fireman?"

"You know who the witch is?" Meeka asked.

"Miss Cowan told me," he said.

"When did you talk to Miss Cowan about the witch?" Meeka yelled.

Why was Meeka yelling at him? He was so sick of her being angry all the time.

"Would you stop yelling at me?" Logan yelled back. "Miss Cowan and I are on your side. Nobody else seems to care. Be great if you could be nice to us for a change. Perhaps you could stop lying so much as well!"

There was silence all around.

Brody coughed. "Is there somewhere we could go? Somewhere where the witch won't find us and the Fireman won't see us? We definitely don't want the Fireman to see us. Especially you kids. Trust me. He's not good with kids."

"Miss Cowan's house is over here," Nate said, pointing.

"Great. Lead on," Brody said.

The front door was unlocked. Poet followed everyone inside. They all went into the lounge and Brody put Miss Cowan on the couch.

Brody Bankston could not be her brother. They looked nothing alike. At all. And he was Brody Bankston, for crying out loud!

As they walked in, everyone gasped, one by one, at all the colours jumping around the room.

"What's wrong?" Brody asked, still looking at Miss Cowan. He was trying to shake her awake.

"It's so colourful in here." Poet smiled as she looked around. "It's the exact opposite of Miss Cowan." It was beautiful. She had no idea what was going on or why the great Brody Bankston would claim to be Miss Cowan's brother, but she knew interior design. This place was funky.

Brody glanced around. "It's not that colourful, not by Tessa's usual standards." He looked back at Miss Cowan.

"She's lost a lot of weight." He shook her shoulder. "Tessa."

Tessa. That was a nice name. Didn't fit Miss Cowan. Poet had thought she was probably a Mabel or an Edith. Was she really a completely different person? Why?

Meeka was standing alone, hugging herself. Poet went over and put her arm around her. What was wrong with her? And what was wrong with Meeka's parents? Couldn't they see she needed them?

Lia came and crouched in front of Meeka, and Meeka collapsed into her arms.

Jason stared at Meeka, his brow creased. He looked worried. Of course he cared. How could Logan say nobody seemed to care about Meeka? They all cared.

"What's going on, Brody?" Jason asked.

"Well, she's out for a while. When she goes like this there's only a few ways to bring her round."

"That's not what I mean," Jason said.

Brody looked at him and half-smiled.

"Sorry, Jason. At this point, you know as much as me. I thought Tessa was teaching some financier's kid. She's been lying to both of us. She never lies to me, so it must be something drastic. I was so surprised to see Meeka in the car with you, Jason. Maybe she knows something," he walked over to Lia.

He put his hand on Meeka's head. "Or should I say Captain Happy. Seeing as I gave you that name, I should be allowed to use it. Me-heartie."

Chapter Sixteen:
The Truth About Meeka

Poet's brain went on full alert mode. Did Meeka know Brody Bankston?

"What?" Meeka let go of Lia and turned to face Brody. "You're Captain Hook? No way!"

"I couldn't believe you didn't recognise me in the car. I know it was a while ago and I had a beard and all that," Brody said.

"All that! You were blond with long hair tied up in a man bun and pirate beads dangling everywhere. Especially in your beard. And you had a patch over one eye!"

Woah! Meeka jumped around like crazy. She hadn't smiled like that since Poet had arrived.

"You do remember," Brody said. "They made me dye my hair black for the movies. Makes my blue eyes pop or something stupid like that. Do you still have the sword I gave you?"

"Of course. I keep it on the wall in my bedroom. How could I not know it was you? You saved my life," she said.

"What!" Lia and Jason both yelled out, their backs straightening like elastic pulled twang-tight.

"What is she talking about, Brody? How do you know Meeka?" Jason's eyes were popping, and it wasn't because of the colour of his hair.

"I know her through Tessa. She's known Meeka for years."

"What does she mean, you saved her life?" Lia interrupted.

"Oh, it was nothing," Brody said. "She was nine or so." He turned and looked at Andrew. "You were taking some time off like you do every year around this time. Tessa always struggled with your need to get away. She's more into having a memorial ceremony. Sorry she was so rough on you."

Andrew flinched.

"Anyway," Brody said, turning back to Lia, "Tessa called me and said Meeka had taken the rope netting down off the side of the tree hut, but the ladder had fallen down too."

Jason shook his head. "What tree hut?"

"You never saw the tree hut Walter had the gardener build?" Brody said. "You couldn't wait to show them, Meeka."

"I changed my mind. I wanted it to be a hiding place. Walter thought I told them, but I never did," Meeka said. "It's up high, so Mum and Dad never noticed it. I love them, but they are always in a rush."

It was almost funny, seeing Jason look so stunned. He normally knew what to say. Lia didn't look any better.

"That's why you took the sides down," Brody said. "So it would be hidden. Anyway, to cut a long story short, Walter couldn't climb, so Tessa called me in to help. I made her and Walter belay me, so I could carry Meeka down.

"He was doing a play as Captain Hook," Meeka said, "He came in his costume and called me Captain Happy, so I wouldn't get scared. I fell..."

"...and I carried her down and it was all fine." Brody smiled.

Maybe Lia missed the part about Meeka falling...

"She said she fell," Lia said.

Oh, no. Here we go.

"How far did she fall?" Jason asked with his hand over his face.

"Only a few feet. I caught her. No problem. I went back to my pirate ship and Tessa took her to a climbing wall and taught her about rock climbing. They went every day for the whole two weeks Andrew was away."

"I thought I'd taught her to climb," Jason said, his voice flat like a pancake.

"Diana told me not to tell you about my climbing and the tree hut. She didn't want to worry you," Meeka said. "But I wanted to keep rock climbing, so I asked you to take me and let you teach me all over again."

"Who's Diana?" Logan asked.

"She was the manager for years and years, before Gillian," Meeka said. "She was wonder-tastic, but she had to leave last year when her husband got a job in Ireland. It was her and Walter's idea for Tessa to come stay whenever Andrew was away. She's been coming forever."

"Diana talked about getting a friend of hers to come help with Meeka when Andrew went on leave. I never met her, but Diana loved her. She came every year," Jason said. "Did you not meet her, Lia?"

"I did, the first time she helped," Lia said. "She was lovely. And competent. After the first year though, my tour was always scheduled at the same time as Andrew's leave, so I never saw her again. But Diana talked to me about her every year." Lia waved her finger at the couch. "She looked and acted nothing like Miss Cowan."

"Why didn't you tell me?" Andrew asked.

"You deserved a holiday Andrew. You do so much for Meeka. For all of us. I didn't want you to have to think about it. Diana felt the same. And her friend was a police officer, so I felt very safe leaving Meeka in her care."

"Miss Cowan's a teacher though," Abby said.

"She is now," Brody said. "Our dad is a cop and she always thought she wanted to do that too. But after three years she resigned and went back to train as a teacher. Said Meeka made her miss kids too much. You probably need to know that Walter, your security guard, is our uncle. That's how Diana and Tessa met. Years ago, Walter invited Diana and her husband to come to our family dinner and Tessa and her became like sisters almost straight away."

"I need to sit down," Jason said.

"Me too," Lia said.

"Me too," Andrew said.

They went over to the breakfast bar and sat on the stools.

Hmmm. That was a huge breakfast bar. You could sit ten people there. Classy-looking too. How'd they get it so big without looking clunky? Oops, what was Jason saying?

"Why didn't you tell me you knew Meeka then?" Jason asked.

"I didn't know you were *Walter's* Meeka's dad. Walter never told us who he worked for because he wasn't allowed to as part of his contract. He said you were in the finance industry. He called you guys, 'The Parents'. Never once said your names. And Tessa never told me she'd met you Lia. Walter and her always told me Meeka's parents were so boring I'd never want to meet them. They must have figured I'd go crazy if I knew you were Meeka's parents. Tessa's better at secrets than I thought."

Was he kidding? She was an expert at secrets. Look at her. Even Meeka hadn't recognised her and she's known her for years.

"We do have a very strict confidentiality agreement. She had to sign it before she came to work with Diana," Lia said.

"That's right, I remember now you saying your sister was teaching a girl called Meeka," Jason said. "Seemed a strange coincidence but I never gave it much thought after you told me her parents were the exact opposite of me and Lia. Boring financiers. Can't think of anything worse."

Meeka was standing by the couch, staring at Miss Cowan, her face beaming. "I can't believe it's Tessa. She's been here the whole time."

"Well, that's all makes some sense. In a very crazy way," Steve said. "But who's the Fireman?"

Thank you, Dad. I'd forgotten about the Fireman. He sounds bad.

"You know, that's quite a story," Brody said. "He's someone who hurt Tessa a lot when she was about Meeka's age. I don't want to scare anyone yet until Tessa can tell us exactly what she knows about him."

He looked over at Miss Cowan.

"I need to make her talk about what she saw straight away, or she'll stuff it down in her subconscious and it'll take weeks for her to get it out. I know it's important for you to know what she saw, but it's just as important for her to be the one talking about it."

Poet stood up a bit straighter. Subconscious! That's what her science project was about. This could be really useful.

"That's not acceptable, Brody. You need to tell us now," Jason said.

"If the kids are in any danger, we want to know right away," Lia said.

"I agree," Abby said.

Brody put his hands on his head. "The witch has left? With a policeman?"

"Gillian, her name is Gillian," Lia said, frowning. "Yes, she left. But she'll be back at one to take Logan and Meeka to the police station. The police officer is not coming back here."

Brody's hands dropped to his side and he smiled.

Poet's heart skipped a beat. He was so handsome when he smiled.

"Great. We don't need to be out of here until one then," Brody said. "We have some time. I promise to tell you about the Fireman if Tessa won't, but I believe you need to hear it from her. She seemed desperate to tell you."

Steve stood up and went to look at Miss Cowan. He lifted her arm and let it fall, he checked her eyes.

"She's out to it for a while though Brody. She was in a lot of distress. And you sure gave her a shock appearing like that."

"That was a bit stupid," Brody said. "But I was just as shocked."

"Jason, Lia," Steve said. "Tessa or Miss Cowan needs a bit of space to recover. We could all leave and come back when she's ready to talk."

"If Brody's not going to tell us, we're not leaving," Jason said. "Not until someone tells us what's going on."

"That's for sure," Andrew said.

"She'll probably freak out though," Brody said, "seeing all of you. She's going to feel terrible about the things she said. It'll be quite overwhelming for her."

"I know," Nate said from the other side of the breakfast bar, "why don't we all sit down here so she can't see us, while Brody, you talk to her over there and get her to explain what's going on."

Jason Whitley and Lia Castaneda crouching behind a breakfast bar? Even Poet thought Nate was being a bit too hopeful.

"I don't think so," Brody said, smiling. "For one thing, I couldn't trick Tessa like that. She would kill me."

"She's been tricking us for the last few months. It's the least you can do," Andrew said. "She knows something that we all need to hear. And I'm so confused and angry I wouldn't notice if I was sitting on scorpions. Let's go with Nate's idea, Jason. Lia and Abby, if you don't want to, we can tell you everything she says later."

"No way am I missing out!" Lia said.

"Me neither," Abby said. Steve smiled at her.

Brody looked at Logan. "Okay. I guess it could work. I'll need some help with asking questions. You're Logan aren't you?"

"That's right," Logan said.

"I heard about you from Jason. Sounded like you've talked to Tessa a bit. How about you sit with me and ask questions whenever she says something nobody will understand?"

Poet sighed. Logan got all the good jobs.

"Meeka has to sit with her parents," Logan said. "She might need them."

Poet looked at Meeka. Was she shaking?

Lia stared at Meeka and then turned to Jason.

"We need to do this, Jason," she said.

Jason put his arm around Meeka's shoulders, and she winced.

"What's wrong?" Jason asked.

"The witch squeezed her shoulders so hard they're bruised. She's really sore," Logan said.

"What? Gillian hurt Meeka? No way!" Poet said.

Lia pulled out the collar of Meeka's top and looked at her shoulders.

"It's true." A tear rolled down her check.

Jason looked at Meeka. "When did you stop trusting me, Meeka?"

Meeka looked at her feet. "When you were never here."

Jason wiped his eye. "I can't believe Gillian did that to you. I'm so sorry."

"Miss Cowan said she always tried to make sure Meeka wasn't alone with Gillian because she thought she was hurting her. She wanted to tell you, but nobody would listen to her," Logan said.

Jason and Lia stared at the ground, shaking their heads.

"Well, we're listening now," Andrew said and put his arms around Jason and Lia. "Let's sit down shall we?"

"Let's get this done. We need her to tell us what she knows. I'm not having anyone else hurt Meeka again," Lia said.

She sounded mad.

Chapter Seventeen:
All About Owen

Logan wasn't sure what he was supposed to do. Brody
was looking for something in the kitchen drawers. Matches.
Why matches?

"Sorry, Meeka," Brody said. "I'm going to light a match."

Huh?

Brody struck the match and let it burn almost to the end.

"Then I'm going to hold the smoke under Tessa's nose.
She's going to scream and yell some stuff you might find
upsetting because from what Jason's told me, you hate fires
as much as she does. Try not to let it get to you, okay? You
guys need to keep quiet."

Logan looked at Meeka. She looked at him. They both
cringed. Then smiled.

They were still friends. Phew.

"Logan, if you sit on the couch opposite Tessa, she'll have her back to the breakfast bar," Brody said. "Don't mention anything about the Fireman. She needs to remember herself."

Logan stared at Miss Cowan. No, it was Tessa now. This whole thing was mind-jangling. And Tessa's wart had moved again. Would the match thing work? She still looked unconscious. Who was the Fireman?

First match, and no movement.

Second match, and a groan.

Third match, and whoa...

Tessa bolted upright, screaming. "Fire! Fire! Get out. We're all going to die!"

Logan jumped a mile. Thwack! It sounded like someone whacked their head on the breakfast bar. He hoped it was Andrew.

"It's me, Brody. There's no fire. It's all okay." Brody held Tessa's shoulders.

She thumped him in the chest with both hands. "You smoked me! You smoked me! You promised me you'd never do that again. How could you?" she shouted.

Intense. She looked like she could thump hard.

Brody stayed where he was. "I know I promised Tessa, but you were out to it big time. Plus I didn't really smoke you. I smoked Miss Cowan, this ugly, hideous, mean maths teacher who probably deserved to be smoked."

Tessa sat still, staring at him for half a minute.

"Brody," she finally said, then collapsed against him, sobbing.

"Logan, can you get us some tissues please," Brody asked.

Tessa wiped her face with her hands and looked around.

"Logan, you're here. Where are the others? Why am I here and not thrown in a lake full of deadly flesh-eating bacteria?"

That was funny. Not like Miss Cowan at all.

"Don't be such a drama queen," Brody said. "The others were a little upset with what you said, but I convinced them they need to hear you out. They've gone back to their house or mansion or whatever that big building is. When you're up to it, Logan's going to go and get them. Do you remember what you said to them?"

"I know I said some really bad stuff to Mr Whitley," she said, her hands over her face. "And then I said some awful stuff to Andrew." She fell back down on the couch.

"I am in so much trouble, Brody."

"Yep, you are pretty high up there on our 'Are we going to get out of this one alive?' scale. I put you at somewhere around, 'Let's choose the colour of your coffin'."

"I think I'm at 'Dead and Buried'."

Brody smiled at her. "It's not that bad. We've been through worse."

Was that even possible?

"Nope. I've never done anything this stupid. This is the worst ever."

"Why were you so upset? Can you remember?" Brody asked.

"Something bad happened and I couldn't take it any more. What was it?" She closed her eyes. "Brody, I can't remember! Why is this happening?"

"It's okay. You'll remember. You had a shock, that's all. Let's start at the beginning and it'll come back to you."

She pulled her feet up and hugged her knees.

"What are you wearing?" Brody said. "Can you please take those horrible glasses off? And since when do you even wear prissy girl shoes like that? Take them off this fancy couch. Where are your boots?"

"I left them at Mum and Dad's, so I wouldn't be tempted to wear them." She kicked her shoes off. "I'm kind of getting used to heels now."

Brody reached over to her face. "I've got to get rid of this wart. It keeps moving because of your tears. It's hard to focus on what you're saying when you're so ugly and your wart's swimming all over your chin." He picked off the wart, wrapped it in a tissue and put it in his shirt pocket. "I might be able to use that sometime. Have you taken a good look at yourself in the mirror? Why on earth are you dressed like that? I'm having a hard time coping with the colour of your eyes. Your hair? Okay. It's a good wig. But why would you do that to your eyes? I loved your eyes."

"What colour are her eyes normally?" Logan asked.

"They're blue," Tessa said.

"Like mine," Brody said. "But mine are bluer."

"They are not," she said. "I've got the bluest eyes."

They smiled at each other.

"I missed you, Brody."

"Missed you, too. Come on now. Explain yourself."

She sighed. "This is really difficult. You're going to be mad, but please listen and don't get all jumpity."

"What would I get mad about?"

Tessa sighed. "Just listen, okay? I've got a bad headache."

"I'm all ears," he said.

Tessa sighed again.

"Remember the day you got the call that you needed to go catch a plane straight away? They wanted you in Spain to shoot the scenes for your new movie?"

"I remember," he said. "Almost two months ago."

"We were visiting Owen in the hospital, right?"

This was his turn. "Who's Owen?" Logan asked.

"Tessa and I were his guardians until he turned eighteen a few months ago." Brody turned towards Logan. "He's fighting cancer, using an experimental drug. He's doing well. I talk to him every day. Right now he's back in hospital taking the last course. It's exciting he's almost all better."

He turned back to Tessa. She was frowning.

"He is doing well, isn't he?" Brody asked.

"Yes, yes, he's doing great. Awesome says if he keeps getting better at the rate he has been, he'll live to be 586."

"Who's Awesome?" Logan asked. Awesome. Who called their kid Awesome?

"Awesome's our older brother," Brody said. "He's a cancer doctor. Saves so many lives, we call him Awesome. Plus, he has great t-shirts."

"That's awesome cool," Logan said.

Brody smiled. "So, what's the problem, Tessa?"

"The drug. They pulled it. We had to start paying to keep using it. Twelve thousand pounds a month," she said.

Brody jumped up and started pacing. "What? How could they? That's not right. They promised he could complete the course if it was working."

"I know, I know. But they changed their mind and it was in the contract that they could and so we basically couldn't do anything."

"Yes, we could. We could go see them in their fancy glass office and make them change their minds back," Brody was almost shouting.

"Calm down, Brody. You're being all jumpity. It gets worse before it gets better so you need to take a chill pill."

"It gets worse?" Brody asked.

"Well, kind of. Awesome had already been to the drug company and spent three weeks trying to get them to change their mind."

"Why didn't he tell me?" Brody asked.

"This is the worst part. He figured you'd be too emotional. He dealt with the company very professionally. But he failed. And then he didn't want to tell you because you had your movie chance. It's a serious movie you're doing now, Brody. You get to keep your shirt on and say complete sentences. Plus, you get to work with some of the best in the industry, like Mr Whitley. It's going to make you."

"It's only a movie!" Brody flung his arm out to his side. "We're talking about Owen's life. I'd have walked away from it if I could help keep Owen alive."

"Exactly. That's exactly what Awesome said you would do. Walk away from your movie."

"How could you not tell me?" Brody asked, tears in his eyes.

Tessa stared at him.

Logan watched them. She was sending him a message with her eyes. Some kind of twin language. Like they could read each other's minds. Spooky. Maybe that's what Nate and Poet had.

"You did try to tell me, didn't you?" Brody said. "Awesome wouldn't let you. I'm going to kill him."

"Don't be mad at him. He meant well. You wouldn't have been able to change anything except help pay the bill. And maybe you'll have to do that now, because I'm fired for sure."

"Of course I'll pay the bill. But how on earth did Awesome stop you? You've never kept a secret like this from me before," Brody said. "Especially one this important."

"Could you please sit down? I hate it when you hop around like a kangaroo. And my headache's getting worse.

The next part's about Meeka, so Logan might have some questions."

Brody sat on the couch opposite Miss Cowan, wringing his hands.

"Okay," he said. "Hit me with it."

Chapter Eighteen:
Miss Cowan Mystery Explained

Nate felt his Dad rub his back. His mother had died of cancer. Not that he could remember her. He looked at Dad. Yep, he'd have given away his career to save her if he could.

"So we were at the hospital, you got your call, but Awesome had already told us he wanted to speak with us. Remember that?" Tessa asked.

"Yeah, then I told him I had to catch a plane, pronto," Brody said.

"You were excited," Tessa said. "Awesome took one look at you, figured you'd throw it all away if he told you about Owen, so decided not to tell you. But I thought he was keeping something back, so I got it out of him as soon as you'd left."

"How could I have missed that?" Brody asked.

"You were keen on meeting Olivia Bianchi," Tessa said.

"Cole likes her too," Logan said.

That should lighten the mood. Brody was stressing too much.

Brody laughed. "Most guys like Olivia. She's almost as good at practical jokes as you, Tessa."

"So I've heard," Tessa said. "Anyway, I wanted to call you and tell you straight away, but Awesome took my phone off me. When I said I was going to go to the airport to tell you, he snuck up behind me and put a cloth soaked in something over my nose. The next thing I knew, I woke up locked in the cleaner's closet."

"No way!" Logan said. Wow. Wicked! Were doctors allowed to do that? "Awesome sounds great! He wouldn't really do that would he?"

"She's not lying." Brody said. "He didn't want me to know."

"I think he's sick of seeing you in Jungle Wars. The teenagers on his ward play it over and over," Tessa said.

"When it first came out, the nurses strung a rope up in the cafeteria for him to use. Like Tarzan. He's never forgiven me."

Nate heard Logan laugh. That was funny.

"What happened next?" Brody asked.

"I was locked in the cupboard for six hours until your plane left. Awesome kept away. When I was finally let out, I headed straight for his office. Guess who was there?"

"No idea. Hopefully Awesome in full body armour, and a bat to protect himself from you. She's a mean fighter, Logan."

"No, I am not," Tessa said. "Dad stopped me from fighting with you guys when I was five because you all cried so much."

"Very funny. Glad to see you're starting to feel better," Brody said. "Who was in the office?"

"Uncle Walter and Violet. And Awesome, looking pitiful with his, 'You've got to help or my heart's going to break' look," she said.

"I hate that look. Why were they there?" Brody asked.

Nate heard someone stand and walk over to the breakfast bar. Next minute Brody appeared in the kitchen and leaned against the fridge.

"Don't mind me, Tessa. I'm still feeling a bit jumpity. You keep facing Logan and then you don't have to watch me moving around. But speak up a bit."

Clever move. They wouldn't miss anything she said now.

"Why were Walter and Violet there?" Brody asked.

"Walter was sure he and Violet were going to get fired and they were worried about Meeka. Turns out they were right. They were both fired three weeks ago."

"Why?" Brody asked.

"Violet for some minor thing. She knew it was coming. Gillian had already given her two warnings. Walter for not having the security cameras going when one of the cars here was stolen."

"The Bugatti," Logan said.

"A Bugatti was stolen? And Uncle Walter was blamed?" Brody asked.

Brody sure sounded like he didn't believe it. His whole face said, 'No Way'.

"But Uncle Walter prides himself in his security. He wouldn't let something like that happen," Brody said.

"Meeka was upset about Walter being fired," Logan said.

Nate watched Meeka bury her face in her arms. Was she crying? Or hiding?

"Of course she was," Tessa said. "But it was what they both expected. They didn't care about that, but they were super worried about Meeka. Violet told me how sad Meeka was and how she'd seen Meeka a couple of times with a red slap mark on her face after she'd been in with Gillian."

"That's terrible," Brody stepped over to Lia, bent down, put his hand over her mouth, and shushed her.

Had anyone ever shushed Lia Castaneda before?

"Where are you, Brody?" Miss Cowan asked.

He stood up. "Just dropped something. So you decided to dress up as a mean old teacher and make everyone miserable? Especially Andrew. You freak the poor guy out. Seems you look like his nasty high school teacher."

He winked at Andrew.

"Is that what his problem is? How do you know that?"

"He was talking about you in the car on the way over. Said a lot of unfriendly stuff. If I'd known it was you he was talking about I would've opened the driver's door and pushed him out."

"Thanks. But even if I remind him of some monster from his school years, it's still not professional to avoid talking to me."

Bet Andrew was feeling stink right now. Poor guy. He should've talked to her.

"Don't sulk. You shouldn't give him a hard time about how he copes with his family's death. Losing someone in a terrorist attack is a lot different to losing someone to illness."

Andrew stared at Brody and mouthed a "Thank you."

"I know that," Tessa said. "I should never have said those things. I admire how Andrew has put his life back together. And looking after Meeka when seeing her growing up must remind him of everything he's lost. Apparently, he somehow managed to come out of it all as a really nice guy too. According to Meeka, anyway. That hasn't been my experience."

Andrew's shoulders sunk so low they almost touched the floor.

"I must have been stressed to say all that stuff to him," Tessa said. "But I can't remember what made me so upset."

"Don't worry Tessa. You'll remember. One thing at a time."

"Okay, but it would be good if you could not make me feel any worse about how I treated Andrew."

"Sorry, Tessa. It's a lot to take in. Puts my mind in a spin, seeing you like that. Why did you dress up like a mean old teacher?"

"None of this was my idea," Tessa said. "Walter, Violet, and Awesome came up with the plan. Walter said there was an opening for a teacher. Getting the job meant I could do some snooping around and see what Gillian was up to while keeping Meeka safe. Awesome said, it's good pay and comes with a house so I could use the salary to help with paying for Owen. Awesome planned to pay for his meds from his savings so anything I could give would help."

"He should've told me," Brody said.

"Get over it, Brody. There's much bigger problems," Tessa said.

"So let's go back to why you had to dress like that and be so awful," Brody said.

"Violet said I'd never get the job if I looked like a friendly pixie. Gillian fired the last teacher because she was a lovely person who was friends with Andrew. Gillian has her eyes set on marrying Andrew. Well, that's what Violet thought. She said any female was a threat."

Nate leaned forward and looked at Andrew. He went red in the face.

"Any female except one who looked like an ugly mean teacher, of course." Brody shook his head at Andrew.

"He does attract the glamorous kind. Perfect-looking women. You've probably met a few now," she said.

"They're not all they're cracked up to be." He looked at Lia and cringed. "Sorry," he mouthed.

She frowned at him.

"It was so hard. I almost blew it the first day. If Violet hadn't still been here, I'd have only lasted five minutes," Tessa said.

"Why?" Logan asked.

"You'll laugh, Logan."

"We could all do with a laugh right now," Brody said. "I mean, Logan and I could sure do with a laugh."

"The day I arrived, Andrew and Meeka were acting out a scene from 'The Hunchback of Notre Dame'. He had a pillow stuffed in his back and he was pulling the most hideous faces. He was the ugliest Quasimodo you've ever seen." Her voice trailed off into a happy sigh.

Brody looked at Andrew and mouthed, 'How could you?'

"Quasimodo's her all-time favourite story character, Logan," Brody said. "You must have fallen in love with him straight away, Tessa."

"Nope. I managed to keep hold of my heart. Just."

"Shame," Brody said. "Imagine what disturbing looking kids you'd have, a mix of Quasimodo and the Principal of Death."

He pulled an ugly face.

Cole and Poet covered their mouths to hide their giggles, while Andrew put his hands over his eyes.

"I'm going to regret telling you this, aren't I?" Tessa said.

"For the next five years at least," Brody said. "So what happened when you saw your dream Quasimodo? Was he hanging off a bell rope? There's a spare rope in the hospital cafeteria if he needs it."

Brody sure was funny.

"It didn't matter what he was doing. It was me. I started laughing and quoting lines from the play. Lucky Violet caught my eye and frowned, because Gillian was staring at me like she had stepped in slime. Violet shook her head and I stopped mid-sentence and said in the snootiest voice, 'I don't believe in frivolous activity like this.' Can you believe it? What a dork. I'm the master of frivolous activity."

Brody looked at Meeka and they both nodded.

"My head hurts," Tessa said. "I'm going to get something to eat. I'm starving."

"No, no. You sit there. I'll find you something," Brody signalled her to stop.

"Oh," she said. "I forgot. There isn't anything."

Brody stood still, and then opened her fridge and her cupboards.

"There's no food here at all," he said. "Why is there absolutely no food in your kitchen, Tessa Marie Bankston?" he asked.

"Don't be mad," she said.

"Don't be mad? You look like a World Vision ad and you tell me not to be mad? There's not a single bit of squishy cuddle left on you."

"I don't mind about losing the squishy part. It's just Violet was here when I started. She offered to feed me so we'd have an excuse to catch up with each other. So, I agreed to giving all my pay except for petrol to Awesome for Owen's treatment. Then Awesome looked so stressed I didn't want to tell him I needed to keep more money when Violet was fired."

Brody shut the fridge door and leaned his head against it. "What have you been eating then?"

"Oh, I have some pasta," she said. "And Violet sends me a food parcel once a week."

"That's the parcels Meeka mentioned." Logan said.

"Yep. You thought they were drugs, didn't you?" she said.

Sure did!

"Maybe," Logan said. "At the start."

"But Tessa, a bit of pasta and a food parcel from Violet once a week isn't enough."

"Rory and I survived on pasta all through university," she said.

"Who's Rory?" Logan asked.

Chapter Nineteen:
The Bugatti

It went silent. Nate wished he could see what was going on with Tessa. It sure was hard to follow. First there was Owen, the kid with cancer they were guardians for. Awesome was their older brother and a doctor. Walter, the security guard, was their uncle. Violet was the cook. Diana, Tessa's friend, was the old manager. Who was Rory?

Brody's face was clouded over.

"You say, Brody." Tessa sounded tragic.

Brody looked away and put both hands on his head. His shoulders sank. He turned back around, his eyes shut.

"Rory was Tessa's husband. They were married for five years before he died of cancer eight years ago. Owen was Rory's little brother and his only living relative. He was only ten when Rory died, so Rory left him in our care."

He paused for a second, opened his eyes and looked at Andrew.

"Every year on the anniversary of Rory's death the three of us visit his grave and go out for lunch and tell each other stories about him. In the evening, we go home and our whole family gets together and talks about Rory and remembers all the good times we had with him. And everyone loves on Owen and Tessa. We have photos of him all over the place. We talk about him a lot."

"You didn't need to tell Logan all that," Tessa said.

Brody looked over to where she was sitting.

"I, err, got a bit emotional. Sorry. I thought it important for An—for Logan to understand why you got so mad at Andrew for going away every year. That's all."

"I shouldn't have got mad, Brody. People are entitled to grieve however they need to. Everyone's different. It's none of my business. I don't believe I said all that stuff."

Andrew leaned back against the cupboard, his hand over his eyes.

"Sorry Tessa, I didn't mean to make you feel bad about it. Let's get back to what we were talking about." Brody looked around. "Food, we were talking about food. I'm upset about you not eating enough, Tessa."

"Don't worry so much about me. I have another source."

"What?"

"I don't want to say now. I'm embarrassed enough."

Andrew opened his eyes. "Where?" he mouthed.

"Please tell me where, Tessa," Brody said. "I'm worried about you."

"Oh, all right. Promise not to tell anyone, Logan," she asked.

"Cross my heart," Logan said.

Nate and Poet crossed theirs too. Brody pointed at everyone else and mouthed, 'What are you doing?'

"I steal food from Quasimodo's place."

"From Andrew's?" Brody asked.

Andrew mouthed, "How?"

"How?" Brody asked.

"At night, when he's asleep. Mostly."

"Mostly at night or mostly asleep?" Brody asked.

"Mostly asleep. Afraid he's got better muscles than you, Brody."

Brody slapped his forehead. "I don't believe this."

"It's true. He does. I could see by the light of the fridge when he came out for a snack."

Andrew was smiling.

"Where was she?" Jason mouthed.

Brody shook his head.

Everyone nodded.

"Where were you?" Brody asked, looking at the ceiling.

"Hiding in the broom cupboard. I wouldn't have fit if I hadn't lost so much weight. He has a lot of cleaning equipment."

"You seem to have a thing about cleaning cupboards," Logan said.

Tessa laughed.

She had a nice laugh.

"Tessa, the man is a bodyguard and a sharpshooter. If he'd spotted you, he'd have killed you on the spot," Brody said.

"Trust me, Brody, there was nowhere he could hide a gun. He was only wearing these boring grey boxers. He needs to brighten up a bit."

Andrew was pinching the bridge of his nose and shaking his head.

"Well, he could've knocked you out and asked questions later," Brody said.

"I'd have liked to see him try," she said.

Brody took a deep breath and looked Andrew up and down.

"Fair point," he said. "You'd have probably knocked him out cold."

"Beat you last time," she said.

"I let you win. Dad said I had to. Anyway, we're not talking about me. We're talking about you stealing food from a known master of self-defence."

"Brody, I was hungry. I had no money, and no one was going to ask me around for dinner. They don't even ask me to morning tea. They all loathe me. Quasimodo can cook a six-course meal with one pot and a wooden spoon. It takes me ten pots and a chainsaw to make half a cup of chewy rice. Can we please move on?"

There were a lot of pots in her sink.

"Whoa, grouchy!" Brody said. "When was the last time you ate?"

"Last night, at the hospital. One of the nurses found me a soggy sandwich. Quasimodo's fridge is much better."

Andrew reached into his pocket and pulled out a protein bar. Brody took it and read the label.

"I have a protein bar in my pocket. Chocolate free." He threw it to Logan.

Chocolate free? Come on, Logan. Ask the question.

"Did you take the brownies from Andrew's freezer?" Logan asked.

That wasn't the question.

"No, she wouldn't do that," Brody said. "She's allergic to chocolate."

That's what Nate wanted to know.

"True?" Logan asked. "Allergic or intolerant?"

Show-off.

"Full-blown allergic. Anaphylactic fit, needing-an-adrenaline-shot and rush-to-the-hospital kind of allergic fit," Brody said. "She's almost died a couple of times."

"Wow!" Logan said.

"Not much fun," Miss Cowan said. "But I did take the brownies."

"What?" Brody said. "Why?"

"For the kids in Awesome's ward. I told them Quasimodo had baked just for them. They loved them. They must be good, because only two of them threw up afterwards."

"Why did you leave the empty container in the freezer?" Logan asked.

Nate had wondered that, too. Mum hated it when they did that.

"I was messing with Quasimodo," Tessa said. "His freezer is so organised, I didn't want him to suspect anything too soon. He would've noticed if the contents of his nicely stacked freezer weren't in a straight line any more."

That was true about Andrew. Mr Tidy.

"I've had fun moving things around in his place. You should see how baffled he looks. It's almost as good as his Quasimodo face."

Brody stared in her direction.

Something was going on with his face. Was he talking to her telepathically?

"You didn't!" he said.

"Don't tell me you didn't while you were away. I've seen Jason put his keys down and tell himself out loud he was putting them there. He's even walked back into the room to check they were where he put them."

Jason tilted his head to one side. His eyes looked kind of squinty.

"Never mind," Brody said. "Let's move on."

"No way!" Logan said. "What did you do?"

Tessa laughed. "I'll tell this one, Brody."

Brody turned and leaned his head on the cupboard.

"Our dad's a cop. Once, when we were your age, he was so annoyed at something we did, he put us in a jail cell for ten minutes. But then he was called out on an emergency, so we spent the whole day in the cell with this really nice jewellery thief. He spent the day teaching us how to pick pockets. It was a lot of fun. We still keep in touch with him."

"Was he the one who told you how to break into the safe?" Logan asked.

"Exactly," Tessa said. "We don't do safe robbing normally. But we do like to lift the occasional key from annoying people's pockets and stuff like that. For a bit of fun."

"You lifted Andrew's car key yesterday!" Logan said. "When you fell against him."

"Yep. I was so mad he wouldn't talk to me. I didn't even know what I was doing. One minute I was talking to him, the next I'm standing in his garage with his keys in my hand. What about you, Brody? Please tell me you've been lifting Jason's keys."

"Of course not. He's not annoying. I have nothing but respect for him."

"But he's still a good target. Maybe if you lift his keys a few times he'll learn to take notice of what's going on around him instead of trying to make everyone happy all the time. I know he feels guilty about being away from Meeka so much, but he doesn't understand that all she needs is some time where they can talk," Tessa said.

Now Jason was leaning his head against the cupboard with his eyes shut.

Brody turned back around. "Stop there, Tessa. What are you doing?"

"I'm coming over there to see if you're telling me the truth."

Brody put both hands up.

"Okay, okay. I did lift Jason's keys a few times and put them in strange places, to pay him back for his Olivia Bianchi joke. Are you happy? Would you please sit down?"

"Who's grouchy now?" Tessa said. "It's not like Dad will ever know."

"I'm not worried about Dad right now," Brody said.

Jason was staring at Brody, his arms folded, his face tight.

This was funny. But it was wasting time.

"Um, so, um," Logan said.

Come on, Logan. Don't start laughing now. Jason will never forgive you. Change the subject.

"So you went to the hospital last night," Logan said.

"Yes, to update Awesome, Violet and Walter with what you knew about Gillian," Miss Cowan said.

"What do you know, Logan?" Brody asked, his hand on the back of his neck.

"She's heading up some kind of crime ring. She's receiving credit card skimmers in the mail, and I think she's keeping an eye on the neighbourhood with her telescope and letting thieves know when people aren't home."

"Good deduction, Sherlock," Tessa said. "I thought that too. Well done. I have some photos of her using her telescope. Always looking down the hill, never at the sky. Always in daylight. And always a couple of hours before a car is stolen."

"Wow," Brody said. "That's circumstantial, but you might be onto something. But heading up a crime ring?"

"She's replaced all the staff with her own people, Meeka's parents are never here, and she's dazzled Andrew with her charms so much, she could keep him busy for months. Meeka is her only obstacle."

"But what does she have over Meeka that makes her keep quiet about how Gillian treats her," Logan said.

"I had an idea about that. It was the Bugatti. It was never stolen. I met up with Meeka's cousin Sofia two nights ago. Sofia and Meeka took the Bugatti for a joyride, and Sofia crashed it. Gillian had the security tape of them taking it in her safe."

Nate watched Meeka slump down even lower on the floor.

"You're kidding! Why wouldn't Meeka say anything?" Logan asked.

"Because Sofia begged her not to. She's in a lot of trouble with her parents and one more stunt like that would mean they'd shift her to a stricter boarding school. She was desperate. She felt bad when I told her though how difficult it's been for Meeka to keep her secret. She's said she'd go home and confess all to her parents. I hope she does."

Everyone looked at Meeka. Jason lifted her face up so they could see it. It was wet with silent tears. Meeka nodded.

Lia put her arms around her.

"But I don't get how Gillian was using the tape," Logan said.

"She was using the threat of telling Jason and Lia about the Bugatti to force Meeka to go along with all the tests and schoolwork she was making me teach. That was her plan all along, to send Meeka to boarding school. I snooped in her office the other day and found out that the tests she's making me give Meeka are entrance exams to different boarding schools."

"Didn't Meeka realise?" Brody asked.

"I think she's so stressed she's not thinking clearly. I went to check the safe was shut late last night and I heard Meeka in Gillian's house. She told Gillian she was going to tell her parents about the Bugatti but Gillian got nasty. She told Meeka the insurance wouldn't pay for the Bugatti repairs if they knew Meeka was at fault, and that would make Jason super angry. Gillian said Jason was doing so well in his career and Meeka was a nuisance who got in his way. Then she said that Lia was planning to go on tour as soon as possible and didn't even notice Meeka when she was home."

Jason and Lia both stood, eyes as wide open as their mouths.

Nate signalled them to sit down, but they didn't see him. Tessa still hadn't talked about the Fireman.

Brody put his hand on their shoulders, they looked at him and he mouthed, 'Sit down!'

They did. Thankfully.

Logan had a coughing fit.

Quick thinking, Logan. That should hide the noise.

"Wow. That's almost unbelievable." Brody left the kitchen.

"I know, and they'll never believe me. They all hate me and think I'm the problem. And I have no idea how to get Meeka to tell them herself."

"We'll think of something. We always do. What happened next?" Brody said.

"I went to bed and cried until two. I needed you, Brody. I tried to call you. Where were you?" she asked.

It sounded like she was crying now.

"I was at the premiere of Jungle Wars Two. I'm sorry I didn't tell you I was here. I wanted to surprise you today. When I went home, someone else was living there. That shocked me."

"Yeah, sorry. I had a place to live here, so I rented the house out short-term to help pay for Owen. He's been staying with Awesome when he hasn't been in hospital. You weren't supposed to be back for another couple of months, so I thought you'd never know."

"You rented out our house? I'm sorry. You shouldn't have had to do that. What a mess."

"Thanks, Brody,' she said.

"So how about this morning? What happened today?" he asked.

Chapter Twenty:
The Fireman

Logan watched Tessa rub her temples.

"Let me think. I was tired because I'd cried half the night. I woke up late, a wreck. Didn't eat anything—of course. Remembered I'd made Logan promise not to tell any one anything until lunchtime today. I planned to get Dad to come back and arrest Gillian. But I didn't have any evidence. So … so what did I do then?"

"Take your time," Brody said.

"Okay. It's coming back." she said. "I was thinking about evidence. Something to give Dad reason to take out a search warrant. I remembered Logan saying Gillian had taken the credit card skimmer back to her house and thought if I could see it for myself Dad would have enough proof to apply for a search warrant. Gillian normally visited Andrew in the morning, so, I'd just go to her place while she wasn't there and take a photo of it."

"Good idea," Brody said.

"I walked into the lounge and…"

She grabbed Brody's arm.

"And…?" Brody asked.

"I saw a man talking to Gillian in the kitchen. They couldn't see me. He was saying, 'Keep going Gillian. Not long now. There are other ways to deal with Meeka besides boarding school.' I knew that voice, Brody. I froze."

"And…?" Brody asked.

"I couldn't move. Gillian said, 'I guess so. If we have to.' Then Gillian stood and she saw me and I … I said something about looking for her. The man turned around and stared at me. It was him, Brody. It was the Fireman. I left as fast as I could and ran to the gardener's shed. I would've thrown up if I had any food in my stomach."

"Who is the Fireman? Why are you so afraid of him?" Logan asked.

No reply.

"I think you should tell him Tessa," Brody said.

"He's only thirteen."

"Older than you when it happened. He needs to know if he's going to convince Jason and Lia to listen to you," Brody said.

Whoever he was, he sounded bad. Maybe Logan didn't want to know.

"When I was twelve, one of my friends and I were kidnapped by the Fireman." Tessa's voice was straight and level. No emotion at all. "She was kidnapped because her family was rich. Me, because Dad had been coming down hard on his gang. It was a message for Dad to back off. Her parents paid the ransom for both of us. But the Fireman didn't let her go. He set the building on fire. He made me watch the building burn and listen to her screams as she died. Then he sent me back to Dad with the message, 'Any of your kids, any time'."

Imagine hearing someone screaming as they died! It was like the nightmare Logan kept having lately about Meeka and him. They were trapped in the fire at Hideaway Lodge and there was no way out this time. He always woke up screaming.

Tessa stood up and started pacing. "Brody, the man with Gillian was the Fireman. I'll never forget him. And I froze. All those years of counselling and martial arts training and gun training and whatever else so I'd be ready if I ever met him and I froze. If he'd recognised me, he'd have killed me."

"It was a shock, that's all Tessa. You weren't expecting him. Next time you'll be ready," Brody said. "But there won't be a next time, because I'm not going to let him get near you. All right?"

"It's not about me. If I cared about me I wouldn't be dressed in this hideous outfit, acting like someone who … who…enjoys maths! It's about Meeka. It's always been about Meeka. He's planning on kidnapping her and the kids. Then he'll kill them. I'm sure. We've got to get them out of here."

"I agree." Jason stood.

"Me too," Lia said. "The sooner the better."

Steve and Abby jumped up as well.

Tessa stopped pacing and stared at them, her hands over her mouth.

"Brody James Bankston, what have you done?" she squeaked.

"It seemed like a good idea at the time," Brody said.

Andrew stood.

"Not you too!" Miss Cowan said. She turned to run, but Brody caught her and held her tight.

"I don't know which is more frightening, Brody, to run and be shot by the Fireman or stay and look over there." She waved her arm in the direction of the adults. Nate and Poet stood up as well.

"How could you do this to me?" Tessa looked into Brody's face. "You're supposed to be on my side."

"He is, Tessa." Meeka stood up and walked over to her. "Like you're on my side."

"Meeka, you heard all that too?" Tessa bit her lip.

"I missed you." Meeka hugged her.

"I wanted you to tell your parents." Tessa wrapped her arms around Meeka. "They shouldn't have heard this from me. They don't even like me. Why didn't you tell them? Don't you remember all those times I said your Mum and Dad loved you and wanted to know what was going on with you? I've been telling you that for years."

"I was scared, Tessa. It's the first year I've done Andrew's busy time without you and Walter and Diana. Gillian is scary. Everything's gone wrong."

"I know, sweetheart. I saw that. I tried to stop you ever being alone with Gillian. Even if it meant we had to do all that maths. I am sorry about all the maths."

"I used to like maths."

"I never understood why," Tessa smiled and kissed the top of Meeka's head. She looked up at Lia. "Did you even try to talk to your parents?"

"I didn't want them to send me away to boarding school," she murmured.

"Oh, Meeka." Lia took her from Miss Cowan's arms into her own. "We would never send you away. Everything Gillian told you was a lie."

"We love you, Meeka." Jason held her too. "More than anything."

Andrew came up and crouched beside her. "I'm so sorry, Meeka. I let you down. None of this should've happened."

"You're not mad about the Bugatti?" Meeka asked.

They all shook their heads.

Meeka hugged her dad.

Lia turned to Tessa. "Thank you," she said. "I don't know how we'll ever thank you enough for everything you've done for Meeka. For so many years."

"I'm so sorry for how we've treated you," Jason said.

Tessa nodded and looked at Andrew. "I'm sorry, Quasimodo. Sorry, I mean, Mr Masterton. I know I upset you. I was trying to help Meeka, but I never should've said all that stuff to you."

"This is my fault." Andrew blinked back tears. "I should've seen it happening, but I didn't even give you the time of day. And Meeka being terrorised by Gillian! I didn't have a clue. I'm the one who's sorry, Miss Cowan."

"Please don't call me that. It's not even my name. Tessa's fine."

"Can she call you Quasimodo?" Meeka asked. "You do make a great Quasimodo. When you're being ugly."

Andrew shut his eyes and let out a breath.

"She can call me anything she wants to after all she's done for you. Although I'd be surprised if she ever wants to talk to me again."

"I want to talk to you," Brody said. "This is a very touching moment, but what time did you say Gillian would be back?"

"One o'clock," Steve said. "She wanted to take Meeka and Logan back to the station to give their statements."

"She won't take them there," Tessa said. "It'll be a setup. When I was kidnapped, someone Dad trusted was taking us to school when the car was hijacked. She seemed to do everything she could to help find us and was so upset when my best friend was murdered. But Dad figured out a year later that she was part of the gang who kidnapped us."

"I think Tessa is right," Brody said. "And even if she's wrong, I don't want to be here when this Gillian witch gets back. We need to talk to the police. The real police."

"We should go to the police station," Tessa said.

"Not with Lia. Not a good idea to take her there," Andrew said. "It'll be tweeted before she even gets out of the car. The Fireman will find us for sure."

"I think we should go to the hospital and talk to Awesome," Jason said. "Maybe the police can meet us there."

"Seems a safer place to me," Andrew said. "Gillian's not likely to guess we'd go there. Plus if anyone did recognise Lia, she could say she was visiting someone."

"But you'll have to go unco-nerdo, hon," Jason said. "You too, Brody."

"Unco-nerdo? Is that incognito?"

"Yep," Logan said.

"Unco-nerdo, huh? That's a look I'm getting used to." Brody cringed. "I've even bought a shirt like an accountant would wear."

Chapter Twenty-one:
The Jellybean Man

Sunday Lunchtime

Meeka sat in between her Mum and Andrew at the front of the van. Her parents weren't mad. Tessa was back. Andrew was sorry. Logan was on her side. Surely it was all good now?

Except for the Fireman. Did he really want to kidnap her? To murder her?

Her pulse did a sidestep.

Andrew parked in the corner of the hospital carpark. Meeka turned around to look at the others. Tessa hadn't wanted to get changed in case the Fireman returned before they left, so she still looked like a mean old teacher.

"Brody," Tessa said. "I can't go in dressed like this."

True. She'd probably scare all the kids in the ward.

"Don't worry," Brody said. "I bought you a present in the markets. I was going to give them to you this morning, but you weren't home." He opened his backpack and pulled out some boots with flower patterns and a long colourful skirt with a peacock splashed across the front.

"Those are gorgeous!" Tessa said, and kissed him on the cheek. She jumped out of the van, pulled up the skirt, and then pulled her grey trousers off underneath and threw them in the nearby rubbish bin.

"Never again!" she shouted.

Everyone cheered.

"Oops." She pulled the pants out of the rubbish bin, and then took something from their pocket.

"EpiPen," She showed them the pen before putting it in her skirt pocket. She threw the pants in the bin.

"Never again!" she shouted.

Everyone cheered one more time.

She turned around and looked at Brody.

Meeka knew that look. Even with the wrong colour eyes. Tessa was scheming.

"Brody," she said. "Look at this awful blouse. I can't let the kids see me in this."

"Oh no, you don't." He tugged at his shirt. "This is a brand-new shirt. I bought it from one of those exclusive shops where they sit you down and give you fancy coffee. I've never owned anything this expensive. You are not getting it. You'll give it away to some sick kid or homeless guy."

"Oh," Tessa said, her mouth downturned.

How did she get her face to look that pitiful?

"I promise I'll give it back. It's such a nice shade of blue. But I understand. You don't want to because it'd be obvious my eyes are much bluer than yours if I wore that shirt."

Brody stared at her, his blue eyes tightening.

"What would I wear?' he asked.

"Umm.' She turned around to look at everyone. "Mr Whitley's got a t-shirt on under his shirt. You could wear his t-shirt." She winked at Jason.

Jason shook his head. "I'm being done, aren't I?" he said.

Tessa put two fingers up to her mouth. "If you both took your shirts off, we could have this sorted in a minute."

Poet looked at Meeka.

They both giggled while the famous Brody Bankston took his shirt off and gave it to Tessa.

Tessa had won the bet! She smiled at Brody. "Maybe the girls could have a photo with you. You know, while you're shirtless. They're your biggest fans."

"You're so funny. Absolutely not," Brody said.

Tessa mouthed "I tried" to Poet.

Jason took his shirt and t-shirt off, handed the t-shirt to Brody, and put his shirt on again.

"Nice muscles, Mr Whitley," Tessa said. "I see why Ms Castaneda keeps you around."

"You better call me Jason now you've seen me without my shirt on," he said.

"And anyone who can win a bet like that with Jason can call me Lia. Pay the woman, hon. I think it was fifty quid?" Lia said.

"Thank you." Tessa took the money. "Now I can afford to buy you all meat pies from the café here for lunch. You gotta try them. They're great. Wait a sec. I'll get rid of the hair and eyes and stuff."

She ducked around the back of the van.

"Brody," she called.

"What?"

"I'm too scared to come out."

"Excuse me, please." Brody rolled his eyes and walked behind the van. "You dyed it blue!"

"I was bored. Mean old teachers have no social life. One of the teenagers on Awesome's ward gave it to me because her hair fell out. She couldn't use it."

"It's cute. Let's get this over and done with."

Tessa mumbled something. Brody mumbled back. Meeka thought it was, "He'll like it. He won't think you're a pixie."

A minute later Brody appeared, pulling a woman with short blue pixie hair and blue eyes that popped.

Tessa. About time! The blue hair was offbeat awesome. Meeka could see orange streaks in it. If only Tessa had her blue lipstick as well.

Everyone gasped.

Guess they hadn't ever expected to see Miss Cowan look like so much fun. F. U. N. In capital letters.

"You're kidding me. She's a pixie!" Andrew said. He turned and leaned his arms against the van. "I don't believe it."

What was his problem? Hadn't he always joked that his perfect woman was Tinkerbell?

Men!

Tessa's face fell, and she sniffed.

"I think you look amazing." Abby touched Lia's shoulder and nodded in Andrew's direction as she went past her to hug Tessa. "I love how you look."

"You look beautiful!" Lia said.

Tessa looked sweet. Not beautiful. But who cared? What was the big deal about being beautiful anyway? It took a long time and a lot of money for Mum to look like that. And then she had to cover it all up with a wig and glasses when she wanted to go anywhere without being noticed. Pointless! There were much more important things to do. To be.

"That's so much better. That's how I remember you," Meeka said. "Hope you've thrown those horrible glasses away."

"Me too," Logan said.

"Me too," Jason said, and smiled. "You look great."

"I thought I should keep them." Tessa smiled. "In case I needed to hide from the Fireman."

"We should go inside," Andrew said. "If we want to stay safe."

As Meeka, Tessa, and the others walked into the waiting area, a child ran towards them. Who was that?

Tessa dropped to one knee and the girl threw herself into Tessa's arms.

"You're here! You're here!" the girl shouted. "I thought I'd never see you again."

"Why on earth not?" Tessa asked.

"Because Owen said the witch wouldn't let you go."

"What witch?" Tessa asked.

Surely Tessa hadn't told anyone about Gillian.

"The witch you work with. The one from the North Pole." The girl hopped around, waving her arms in the air. "Owen told us about her. He heard you talking to Awesome last night. She hates children and cooks their fingers for breakfast. She's got this girl called Meeka trapped and is trying all her curses on her before she sells her fingers to the terr … terr … terror … scary people overseas. Last night she turned Meeka into a frog and then a grasshopper and now Meeka doesn't know if she wants to eat leaves or mosquitos for lunch."

She stood still, let out a deep breath and shook her head. "It's a terrible problem."

"Yes, I can see that would be difficult," Nate said.

"Is there any more?" Meeka asked. *This is good. Don't stop.*

"Don't encourage her," Tessa said.

"There's lots more." The girl's eyes widened, and she waved her arms again. "Meeka's father is a famous inventor. He invented jellybeans. Hello! Jellybeans! Isn't that the best?"

"I do like jellybeans," Lia said.

"It's very sad though." The girl's smile turned upside down. "He has to spend most of the year travelling the world to make sure no one is mixing up the colours. Imagine if someone made the pink ones blue, or the red ones black? Disaster!" She stomped her foot.

"That would be a worldwide catastrophe," Nate said.

"It could start a war," Poet said.

"Is that something bad?" the girl asked.

"Very bad," Logan said.

"Good. Then that's why he's never home to keep Meeka safe, because he's busy stopping a war."

"What about the mother?" Cole asked. "Where's she?"

"She's beautiful," the girl said in a dreamy voice. "Almost as beautiful as Lia Castaneda."

She sighed. "Which is why she can't understand why Jellybean Man never wants to come home to her. I mean, she really is beautiful. Have you seen Lia Castaneda? Of course you have! Everybody has! So she wanders around the grounds at night moaning and crying for her Jellybean Man. It's so sad." Her voice wavered. "Especially because she doesn't even see how bad the wicked witch of the North Pole is! Meeka only has two fingers left!"

"That's enough," Tessa said.

"No, no," Steve said. "You need more than two fingers. Unless one's a thumb, of course. What about a bodyguard? Does Meeka have a bodyguard?"

Cole elbowed Steve in the stomach.

"Yes, Quasimodo the Ugly. We all had such high hopes for him. He makes great brownies and he's really really ugly." She pulled a funny face and stomped around in circle. "He scares all the baddies away with his breath."

Andrew rested his forehead on Jason's shoulder.

"He'd have fitted in well with you guys," Brody said, his hand over his mouth.

"We thought so, but he doesn't like you, Tessa." The girl put her arms around Tessa's shoulders. "He's got to like you if he's going to be our friend. But he won't even talk to you. Which is sad for you and sad for us because we wanted to hear his bells. Plus, he'd have been the perfect judge for our Ugly Competition."

She let go of Tessa and looked at the others.

"Do you think you can kill a witch with a bullet? Owen wasn't sure. He was going to Google it today when the nurse wasn't looking. They don't give you Wi-Fi on the wards. Brody, is that you? You should take your hat off. I couldn't tell it was you."

She went over to Brody and he picked her up.

"Missed you, Dakota," he said. "I thought you'd gone home."

"Had a relapse. Got to have a billion more injections starting tomorrow, and I'm going to feel as bad as Owen did when he drank that lemonade we'd put laxative in for

Sergeant Scary, the new security guard, to drink. It sucks, Brody."

"That does suck," he said. "I'm sorry, hon."

Dakota put her hands around his neck and leaned back to look in his eyes.

"I'm scared. Why do I have to do it?" she said.

"Because it'll make you better."

"That's what they said last time," she said. "Are they lying?"

"They're not lying, honey. They're being hopeful. They don't know for sure if it'll make you get better, but they think it might. But they know you won't get better if they don't do anything. You'll get sicker," Brody said.

"Is that right, Tessa?"

"That's how it is," Tessa said and sighed. "Sorry, sweetheart."

"I guess I better stop running away then," Dakota said. "I wasn't doing very well anyway. I'm not allowed out the front door."

"Dakota! There you are!" Someone called from across the room. "You can't keep hiding like that. Awesome is worried sick about you."

"Owen!" Dakota said. "Look who's here."

Chapter Twenty-two:
Owen's Stories

Meeka turned around. A bald, dark-skinned guy, about the same age as Cole, came up to Dakota. He must be the Owen Tessa was talking about. The one who Tessa and Brody had looked after for so long. The one with cancer.

"Brody! You're home. About time!" He gave Brody a hug over top of Dakota.

"You're squishing me!" Dakota shouted. "Look, Tessa's here, with a whole lot of kids who still have all their hair! Isn't it great?"

"I'm so upset!" Owen said, smiling. "Are people still growing hair out in the healthy world? What a waste of money on shampoo and haircuts and all that stuff." He pointed at Lia. "Are you hiding your baldness, Ma'am? I've seen that same wig on old Mrs Grindley. You can be bald here. It's all good. We're having an ugly bald competition soon. If you're brave enough, you can take your wig off and join in."

Then he had a coughing fit.

Which was probably good, because Lia looked like she'd seen an elephant balancing on a fish tank.

Meeka laughed out loud. Poet punched her in the shoulder.

Everyone else was trying not to laugh.

Owen stopped coughing. "Who are all these people?" he asked Brody.

"This is Meeka, and these are Meeka's cousins and aunt and uncle." Next, he pointed to Jason, Lia, and Andrew. "And these are the Jellybean Man and his beautiful wife, and Quasimodo."

Owen's jaw fell. "Did you tell them the story, Dakota?' he whispered.

"It's not a story. You said it was real!"

"Shizz-mah-nizz!" He shut his eyes.

"Don't swear," Dakota said.

"Shizz-mah-nizz is not a swear word, Dakota." He opened his eyes. "I'm sorry, everyone. It was only a bit of fun to take the kids mind off feeling so bad. I didn't mean any harm."

Brody looked at Owen and nodded at Tessa, eyebrows raised.

Owen turned towards her.

"Tessa, don't look so mad. I'm sorry, all right."

"No, it's not all right. You can't go making fun of the people I work for. You don't even know them," Tessa said.

"We don't mind, Tessa," Jason said. "It was funny." He smiled at Owen, who mouthed 'thank you' back.

Tessa had tears in her eyes. "I'm sorry. It's been a upsetting day and this is too much."

Owen bit his lip and stared at Tessa for a half a minute before he spoke. "I'm sorry my stories upset you, Tessa. But please try and understand what it's like for me. Since I've been staying with Awesome I'm spending so much more time here on the ward. He never goes home. And do you know who else is here? Children who are dying! They're all dying, Tessa!" He sniffed. "And do you know what all the girls want?"

Tessa frown disappeared, and her shoulders dropped. "Just one more Lia Casta-bleeding-neda story. Lia Casta-bleeding-neda goes shopping. Lia Casta-bleeding-neda goes out for breakfast. Lia Casta-bleeding-neda has her nails done. Every minute detail about Lia Casta-bleeding-neda's day."

His voice choked with tears. "I'm sick of everything Tessa. I have no control over anything. The only thing I can change is the stories I tell to make the kids smile. And I'm sick of telling stories about Lia Casta-bleeding-neda. I only wanted to make the kids happy without having to make up one more fairy tale about her."

Tessa put her hands behind her neck and sniffed.

Brody hugged Owen, then stood with his arm around his shoulder.

Meeka didn't dare look at her mum.

Dakota spoke up. "He made us all cry yesterday. He said Lia Castaneda went on a motorbike ride with a gang of crocodiles and robbed a grocery store."

"And what did you say, Dakota?" Owen said, pinching the bridge of his nose with his eyes closed.

"I said there was no way Lia Castaneda would go on a motorbike. It would break her high heels."

Owen groaned and opened his eyes.

"So then Owen said she changed her look and went punk with big black boots up past her knees and huge skull and crossbones earrings and she only did rap and she took a chainsaw on stage and she cut the drums in half with it and rode off the stage on her motorbike over the top of everyone's heads. Splat. Blood everywhere!"

Meeka peeked at her mum. She looked like she'd seen the elephant doing somersaults on the fish tank.

"That is crazy awesome. I love it!" Meeka said.

"We all cried," Dakota said.

"Did I hear my name?" A man in white trousers and a dark blue t-shirt with Scooby Doo on the front came up to them. He had a stethoscope and a name badge on a lanyard around his neck. Same blue eyes as Tessa and Brody, but he was older. Awesome. This must be Awesome. Nice t-shirt.

"Tessa, relax. You look like you're going to bawl your eyes out," Awesome said.

Tessa swallowed, and put her hand out. She was bright red.

"I need a minute," she said and walked outside. Lia followed her. Andrew went after them both, probably doing the bodyguard thing. Hopefully Mum wasn't mad about Owen's stories. They were blaze-sonic.

"Brody," the man said, "Nice to see you. Looks like you have something of mine." He held out his arms for Dakota.

"I'm not yours," Dakota said as she fell into his arms.

"While you're in this hospital, you're mine, young lady. And you are grounded. You are not allowed to go past the ward doors. Ever."

"Awesome!" she moaned.

He put her down. "Scat!" he said. "The charge nurse is waiting for you."

"I'll go with her," Owen said. "I think I'm in trouble with Tessa. Big trouble. You need to sort her out, Awesome." He nodded towards the door Tessa went out.

Awesome sighed.

"Sorry about the stories, everyone," Owen said. "I guess we'll go back to Lia Casta-bleeding-neda and what colour shoes she's going to wear. Maybe puke colour. The boys will like that." He went and caught up with Dakota.

"Oh," Awesome said. He looked like he was trying not to laugh. "No wonder Tessa needed a moment. The Lia Castaneda stories. They're quite a hit with the girls. Brody phoned and told me about your morning and who exactly you all are. And about the Fireman. We better get you upstairs. Brody, Tessa should not be outside this long. If the Fireman followed you, he'll shoot her on the spot. You do realise that, don't you?"

Wow, it really was serious. Easy to forget when she was laughing so much.

Brody paled and turned to go outside, but Andrew appeared and opened the door for Lia and Tessa to come inside. Lia had her arm around Tessa.

Phew, Lia wasn't mad. Actually, it looked like they were both trying not to laugh.

It was funny. Lia Castaneda with a chainsaw, singing rap!

Logan and the others were grinning too.

"That's what we needed," Jason said. "A good laugh. But lead the way, ... Awesome, is it? Do you have another name?"

"Sorry." Awesome offered Jason his hand to shake. "Harrison Bankston. Tessa and Brody gave me the nickname Awesome years ago. I keep it because it helps the kids relax around me. It's not nearly as scary as Doctor Bankston. And you must be Jason Whitley, the Jellybean man. You'll need these." He reached into his pockets and pulled out two packets of jellybeans.

"Try not to give more than about three to each child. Otherwise they get a little hyper. The nurses hate that."

"Harrison Bankston." He held out his hand to Steve, Abby, Lia, and then Andrew. "You must be Quasimodo." He stared at Andrew, and then looked at Tessa.

"Tessa, do you know the meaning of the word ugly?" he said with a frown. "Quasimodo here looks like Captain America. I think that's supposed to be handsome."

"He can look ugly. Honest," Tessa said.

"He can!" Meeka said. "Go on, Andrew. Show them your Quasimodo."

Andrew looked at Meeka, then at Tessa.

She mouthed "Please," at him and he … he went kind of gooey.

Nate elbowed Meeka on one side, and Poet the other. Yep, they'd both seen it too. Maybe Andrew did like Tessa!

Andrew's face twisted into a grimace as he hunched over, reached for Meeka, and tickled her.

"Wow! That's incredible!" Abby said.

The kids cheered and Tessa beamed.

Andrew stood up and relaxed his face. Captain America again.

"Happy?" he asked Tessa.

"Very." She smiled at him.

"The kids will go crazy over that Quasimodo," Awesome said. "Let's go."

Chapter Twenty-three:
Chief Inspector Bankston

Upstairs, Meeka and the others followed Awesome into the ward lounge room after he put up a Not Available sign. As Meeka entered, she stopped and stared at the wall.

Mum! Painted wall-size and so lifelike! As good as any of her billboards!

"Who did this?" Lia asked.

"Tessa, of course," Awesome said, looking surprised. "Oh, you know her as the maths teacher. She hates maths. She's more of a language and arts teacher. And PE. Where is she?"

"She went to visit one of the kids." Jason didn't take his eyes off the painting. "Andrew and Brody are keeping an eye on her."

"That woman. I can never keep her in one place. Excuse me," Awesome said.

He was back in a few minutes towing Tessa by her arm. Brody came in with her, but Andrew stayed outside, by the door.

"Stay there, Tessa," Awesome said. "It's not safe for you to wander around. It's not safe for any of you to wander around. You of all people, Tessa, should know to take this seriously."

"I do take it seriously, Awesome. I only wanted to see the kids for a minute."

"No," he said. "Stay here or I'll put you back in the cleaner's closet."

The door opened and Andrew came in followed by another man. He had short grey hair, blue eyes like Tessa and Brody, and wore a plain white collared shirt, jeans, and a casual jacket. He looked relaxed in a scary kind of way. Scarax.

He scanned the room. He wasn't relaxed. He was checking everyone out.

"Bet he's good at our Notice game," Logan whispered.

"Yep," Meeka whispered back.

"Dad!" Tessa said and gave him a hug.

"Why are you always in so much trouble?" he asked.

"Technically, it was Brody's fault," she said and winked at Brody.

Brody pulled her hair. She turned and pinched his nose. He yanked her ear. She stood on his foot.

"Cut that out. Now," Mr Bankston said.

"Sorry," Tessa said.

"Missed you, Dad," Brody said, pinching Tessa's shoulder.

"It's good to see you." He hugged Brody. "Leave your sister alone."

"Sorry, sir. I missed her a lot. How's Mum?"

"She'll be a lot better when the Fireman's behind bars."

"How does she know about the Fireman?" Brody asked, his eyes narrow. "Tessa only saw him this morning."

"I have something to say to you all about that. It'll be particularly troubling to you, Mr Whitley, Ms Castaneda, and Mr Masterton." He shook hands with the adults. "Let me introduce myself. I'm Detective Chief Inspector Bankston, and Harrison, Brody, and Tessa's father. For the last three weeks we've been following someone of interest to you all, especially you kids."

"Who?" Nate asked.

"We've never heard of the Fireman," Logan said.

"But you have heard of Mr Gomander, haven't you?" he asked.

Meeka looked at the others. Their mouths were wide open, like they'd seen the elephant juggling the fish tank.

"What do you know about Mr Gomander?" Jason asked.

"He's the father of Gillian Gomander, who is currently using the alias Gillian Tanner," Chief Inspector Bankston said.

"No way!" Nate said.

"Not Mr Gomander!" Poet said.

"He's Gillian's father?" Logan asked.

"Meeka, by the way you're shaking your head I guess you don't believe me either?" Chief Inspector Bankston asked.

At this point, she'd believe anything. Her elephant was training the fish to jump through a hoop.

"This is going to take a long time if I have to convince you all of each fact in the case. How about you all just listen and assume I'm not trying to trick you," Chief Inspector Bankston said.

"Who's Mr Gomander?" Brody asked.

"He's the man who tried to steal a whole lot of gold bullion off a shipwreck, but these kids stopped him getting away with it," Tessa said.

"Cool," Brody nodded.

Chief Inspector Bankston looked at his watch. "Do you remember Detective Wright?" he asked.

Everyone nodded.

"He was the lead detective in the gold bullion case," Abby said. "Nice man."

"Yes," Chief Inspector Bankston said. "Detective Wright asked me to assist with your case because I'm head of the Criminal Investigations Department, the CID. We deal with a lot of different crimes. After the gold bullion heist went wrong, we kept our eyes on Mr Gomander. He's very much a newbie in the crime scene and easy to keep tabs on. We decided not to bring him in because we hoped he'd get in touch with Gillian. We'd lost track of her about a year ago. She's a known associate of many London criminals, and someone we like to keep an eye on. We thought she would've had the contacts to fund Mr Gomander's salvage operation. When everything went wrong for him we hoped he'd run to her for help, and possibly protection."

"Gillian? She really is a crook?" Lia sat down, shaking her head.

"She's more than a petty crook, Ms Castaneda. She's an experienced criminal and con artist."

"We had no idea," Andrew said. "She's been working with Jason and Lia for the last year. She came highly recommended by the employment agency."

"The agency you hired is a suspected front for a crime syndicate. But it's hard to get evidence. Gillian Gomander is clever. You would never have had any idea," Chief Inspector Bankston said. "Once Mr Gomander telephoned her, we were able to locate her at your home."

"But," Steve said, "why didn't Gillian try to stop them going to Hideaway Lodge that weekend? She would've known about them moving the gold."

"I never told her," Jason said. "It was a last-minute decision, because I wanted it to be a surprise for Lia and Meeka. I'd seen the brochure on Gillian's desk about six months earlier. She'd seemed adamant I shouldn't go but I liked the sound of it and took Lia and Meeka anyway. We had a great time, but Gillian seemed offended that we'd gone so I purposely didn't tell her that we were going again that weekend."

"She knew about the gold all along," Andrew said. "I can't believe how surprised and upset she seemed about it all."

"Me neither." Lia took a deep breath. "So has she been committing crimes while working for us?"

"Some things," Chief Inspector Bankston said. "Car theft, credit card skimming, and printing fake IDs for illegal immigrants. Mostly she was lying low, building your trust in her."

"Lying low!" Lia said. "How is any of that lying low?"

Chief Inspector Bankston rubbed the back of his neck. "It's lying low compared to stealing money from you. If she could win your trust, eventually she'd be able to influence your decision on who you employed as your accounting firm, and then she and her associates would have access to your bank account. That's worth investing a year or two of her life into from her point of view."

Meeka grabbed hold of Logan's arm and stared at Mum. Wig-walloping weasels!

Lia gasped and looked at Jason.

"No way!" he said.

"Had she mentioned anything about your accounting firm? Anything at all? Good or bad?" Chief Inspector Bankston said.

Lia spoke, her voice shaky. "She's always admired them. She even said they were the best firm in the field. But last week soon after I got back from tour, she grumbled about how slow they'd been to pay the house staff while I was away."

"My pay came through on time," Tessa said. "I needed it for Owen's cancer treatment, so I was keeping a close eye on it."

Chief Inspector Bankston nodded. "Sounds like she was beginning to give you some reasons to consider getting a new accounting firm."

"I think I want to throw up," Lia said.

.

Chapter Twenty-four:
Kidnap Threat

Meeka looked at her mum. It was a blow for her. She'd relied on Gillian.

"Maybe you should get some fresh air, hon," Jason said.

Lia shook her head. "No, I'll be fine. I've sung to fifty thousand people feeling sicker than this. Let's hear the rest of it."

"All right," Chief Inspector Bankston said. "Gillian was firmly established in your household. I imagine she was feeling confident. Her father was going to make a lot of money with the gold bullion, and she'd get her share of that. She was managing to steal a few cars, and the police didn't know where she was. Then you went on your last tour, Ms Castaneda, and Gillian started firing people and changing the staff. All this time Walter, my brother, was working for you as your security guard, but he had no idea who Gillian was. We don't talk work when we're together as a rule. He and

Violet came up with this crazy idea for Tessa to spy on Gillian. Nobody told me."

He gave Tessa and Awesome a mop-the-floor-with-you-scary stare.

"I had no idea who Gillian was, Dad," she said. "I didn't even like the idea of spying on her. Except I was worried about Meeka. You know how I feel about Meeka."

"You are a teacher, Tessa. You tried the whole police thing for three years and decided it wasn't for you. I do not ever expect to see you pulling a stunt like this again," he said. "As for you, Harrison, we will talk later."

Awesome cringed. "Yes, sir," he said.

Chief Inspector Bankston shook his head. "I'm just glad you didn't tell Brody."

"They should've told me," Brody said.

"Don't be ridiculous," Chief Inspector Bankston said. "What's your role as Tessa's twin brother, Brody?"

"I don't know. I look out for her," Brody said.

"You do not look out for her. She has a stupid idea. You go along with it. Then you try and save the both of you with your own stupid idea and get even deeper into trouble. Then me or Harrison or your mother rescues both of you. Am I correct?"

"No," Brody said.

His father eyebrows shot up.

"All right. You may be slightly right. We are twins, you know. We're made of the same stardust." Brody smiled at Tessa.

"Exactly. You have one brain between the two of you."

Funny. That was the perfect description for Nate and Poet. Steve and Abby were smiling at each other as if they thought the same thing.

"Well, it's a big brain," Brody said.

"It's got twice as many neurons firing as most people with a whole brain to themselves," Tessa said.

"If you say so," Chief Inspector Bankston said. "Let's get back to Mr Gomander, shall we? His salvage operation failed. He contacted Gillian. We finally figured out where she's been hiding the last year. Surprise, surprise, there's my daughter dressed up as... I don't know what to describe it. Suffice to say I was furious, especially when I realised Walter had given her equipment, the glasses, from my department to monitor what was going on."

"The glasses?" Tessa said. "How did he get them?"

"He made a deal with the tech guy. Once this is all over, apparently you're going on a date with him."

"Eww, no," Tessa said.

Brody burst out laughing.

His father stared at him and Brody's laughter stopped dead.

"I'm sure I can find something you did wrong, Brody," Chief Inspector Bankston said.

Meeka winked at Poet. He'd lifted Dad's keys. Did that count?

"Sorry, sir. I'll be quiet," Brody said.

"Good idea, seeing as I thought you two had promised on your life never to pickpockets again."

Brody looked at the floor.

Chief Inspector Bankston said. "Right, that's what I thought. Back to Mr Gomander. So, angry as I was that nobody had run their little plan past me, I was also excited that we had this opportunity to keep an eye on Gillian. In between Tessa's extremely boring math's lessons, that is."

He winked at Meeka.

They were sooo boring. Gigabig boring.

"So, someone from your team has been watching everything I've been watching?" Tessa's mouth hung wide open.

That's worse than being watched by minders and teachers and parents and staff.

Or maybe not.

"They are high tech glasses, Tessa. The lens is a camera, and the metal strip inside feeds the picture back to our computers." Chief Inspector Bankston turned to Andrew. "Mr Masterton, all my staff love the inside of your fridge. They want your recipes. A few of them would like to marry you."

Andrew chuckled.

Tessa groaned and hid her face in Brody's arm. He mumbled something in her ear and she hit him.

"Ow," he said.

"I thought you were going to be quiet," Chief Inspector Bankston said, frowning at him.

Brody closed his mouth and ran two fingers across his lips like he was zipping it shut. The laughter burst out of his eyes instead.

"Okay," Andrew said. "Why did you not tell Jason or Lia? They should've been told."

"Jason only got back yesterday, Lia a week ago. I didn't have anything definite on Gillian a week ago. I knew how much you trusted her. I wanted proof. Once I heard Logan tell Tessa about the credit card skimmer last night, I figured we had enough to arrest her. I was getting a search warrant organised this morning when the detective watching the tapes from the glasses saw what Tessa saw."

"The Fireman," Brody said.

Chief Inspector Bankston started pacing the room. "I don't know if Tessa told you he was captured and sentenced to life imprisonment for the murder of Erin Grey, Tessa's friend."

He turned and looked at Tessa. "He escaped from prison two weeks ago."

Tessa swayed. "You never told me."

"I know. I'm sorry," he said. "I should have pulled you out and put you under police protection. But my superiors said you were just as safe where you were, with us constantly watching you and you pretty much dressed in disguise. No one expected him to turn up with Gillian."

Tessa's face was white. Andrew stood up and moved to stand by her. "You're safe now." He squeezed her shoulder.

She pressed her hands together and put them to her lips. "Thank you, Andrew."

"I did put someone here as a hospital security guard to keep an eye on you, seeing as you spend so much of your spare time with the kids in Harrison's ward. Although you sure know how to give my man a hard time."

"Sergeant Scary?" Tessa asked. "He's one of your guys? I've never seen him with you before."

"He is one of ours. He was working undercover for a year or so in Wales with some dangerous people. He joined us a month ago. Thought things would be a lot safer here. Until you decided to use him as the kid's plaything. Making up stories for them about 'Sergeant Scary'. The kids gave him such a hard time he said he should have stayed in Wales. And then the laxative in the lemonade? How could you?" Chief Inspector Bankston rubbed his hands together.

Tessa smiled.

He smiled back and shook his head. "What am I going to do with you?"

Tessa shrugged.

"What happens now?" Andrew asked.

"Now we need to put you all under police protection. This is not a safe place for any of you. From what we saw this morning, the Fireman is friends with Gillian. He could've been planning on using his contacts in Europe to convert the coins to cash, even while he was in prison. Now I suspect his plan is to kidnap Meeka or one of the other children as an act of revenge for them getting in the way of the gold bullion salvage plans."

"Are you sure?" Abby reached for Nate, who was standing next to her.

"Not entirely, Mrs Kelly, but it seems likely."

Everyone looked at each other. This was serious. It was like something from the movies. But scarier.

Chief Inspector Bankston continued. "It's also risky for the patients. We'll have somewhere sorted for you by three this afternoon. Then we'll all leave here together. If you could remain here until then, I'll have my men keep an eye on you. Only a few hours of laying low here and everybody will be safe."

Chapter Twenty-five:
Lia Castaneda Revealed

Meeka looked over at the adults sitting around the table in one corner of the room.

They were talking. Well, it was more like whispering. No point trying to eavesdrop on them. Plus, judging from the tears falling down her mother's face, she didn't want to hear anything.

"This is one crazy morning," Cole said.

"Sorry about all you've been through, Meeka," Poet said. "Your cousin and the Bugatti..."

"And Gillian," Nate said.

"And your parents not having a clue," Logan said. "I couldn't believe they didn't know about any of it. Not even the platform in the tree."

"And Andrew not being there for you," Nate said.

"And Miss Cowan being Brody Bankston's twin sister!" Poet said.

Now that was something to smile about.

"She got him and Dad to take their shirts off!" Meeka winked at Poet. They cheered and high-fived each other.

"What about the Fireman?" Nate said. "He sounds dangerous."

"We've got to look out for each other," Logan said. "We can start by telling each other what's going on. I'm sorry I never told you about talking to Miss Cowan—I mean Tessa—on the roof of her house."

"On the roof?" Nate said.

"Tessa likes roofs," Meeka said. "Especially at night. We always used to eat dinner up on the roof when Andrew was away. Logan's right, we need to talk more. I'm sorry I never said anything to anyone about Gillian. I was so scared."

"Well, she's certainly scary," Cole said. "You must have felt so alone."

Meeka wiped a tear from her eye. Next thing she was being squished from all sides by everyone, like peanut butter in the middle of a sandwich in the middle of a paper bag in the middle of a school bag that someone with a really big bum was sitting on.

Poet would have a poem for that.

Meeka wasn't alone. She had good friends.

Now she was sobbing. Stink.

She was being lifted. She opened her eyes.

Dad. He was crying too. And Mum, make-up totally gone, face all wet. Be a great photo.

Of course they cared. They were just a little slow sometimes. Maybe all the spotlights had fried Mum's brains.

And everyone knew you had to be stupid to work with stuntmen.

Poet watched Meeka talking with her parents. She leaned into Nate.

"You two are just like Brody and Tessa," Logan said.

"Made of the same stardust?" Poet asked. It was a nice line, being made of stardust. She'd have to remember that.

"One brain between the two of you," Cole said, smiling at Logan.

"Not fair. I'm super-smart," Nate said.

Owen came in. His face was all red, like he'd been crying too.

What was wrong now? And who had the tissues this time?

"Tessa, look at this," he was almost shouting. Tessa came over and took a letter from his hand.

"What's it say, Tessa?" Brody asked.

Tessa read it to herself than her arm dropped.

"Who was it for?" she asked Owen.

"Kylie," he said. "It's all she's got left to help her through. She loves Lia. And she's so sick. All I want is for her to hang on a bit longer. So I told her I'd send her drawing to Lia Castaneda. I even used her right name and everything. I was sure Lia would send her one of those standard fan letters. You know, something about how much she loved getting her letter and right now she was in Timbuktu but here's some special photos of her, only for fans. That's all Kylie wanted. A couple of photos from Lia Casta-bleedin-neda to hang on her wall and look at while she's trying not to die. Instead of all the ones I rip out of old magazines for her."

"Can I see that?" Lia reached for the letter. Poet read the letter over Lia's shoulder.

Dear Lia Castaneda Supporter,

Ms Castaneda no longer replies to fan mail due to her busy touring schedule.

Kind Regards,

Lia Castaneda's Manager

Gillian. It had to be. Lia would never send a letter like that. She was always talking about how important her fans were.

Lia's face was going all purple and blotchy. What with the tears and the streaky makeup and the wig, she looked almost as scary as mean old Miss Cowan.

A large man opened the door and a nurse came in, pushing a girl in a wheelchair. The man pushed a drip on a pole behind her. They needed help to get all that through the door.

Poet ran over to hold the door.

"Are you sure there's nowhere else you can go?" the man asked the nurse.

"I'm sorry Sergeant Scary. I don't want to get you in trouble. It's only Kylie's not feeling well, and it helps if she can rest by Lia's painting," the nurse said.

"I guess it'll be all right. But not for long. And I've asked you before to not call me Sergeant Scary. That's the kids name for me. Please call me Rosco. Are you still on for this evening?"

He was tall and huge like a bulldozer. "Yes," the nurse said, all gooey-gooey smiling at him. "Half-past five at your favourite pub, The Mellow Hound. Sounds good. I'm looking forward to it, Rosco." She turned to everyone in the room. "Sorry for the intrusion," she said. "Kylie needs to rest a bit."

Kylie coughed. She was a scrawny girl, small, with no hair, tubes everywhere, and big brown eyes like Logan's. Be awful if Logan ever got that sick. Or anyone else.

"Hey, Owen," Kylie said. "Has the mail come?"

"Yeah, but there was nothing for you, Kylie Honeybear. Not today. Maybe tomorrow." Owen took a deep breath.

Kylie's face fell. "It's been ages, Owen. I think what you said to Dakota is right. Lia Castaneda is a fairy tale."

"No no no." Owen dropped down beside Kylie. "That was only me being mean. I thought Dakota had put the laxative in my lemonade, and I was so mad I didn't know what I was saying. Of course Lia Castaneda's real. She's in all the magazines. And she's beautiful and kind and good and wears matching earrings and necklaces, and she's going to write to you as soon as she sees your picture. Promise. Don't give up, Honeybear."

"My bones ache, Owen," Kylie said.

"I know, I know they do baby face. Mine do too."

"I don't think I can wait any longer. I want it all to stop."

"Don't say that, Honeybear. Just … just…I'll get us tickets. Tickets to her next concert. We'll go together. You and me. Soon as you're better." Tears fell down Owen's face.

"You don't even like Lia Castaneda," Kylie said.

"I do. I only pretend I don't to annoy Dakota," he said. He put both his hands on his chest. "I know all the words from every song. Name me a song, and I'll sing it."

Kylie laughed, then coughed. "You sound terrible when you sing Lia's songs. You've only learned them because I forced you to."

"That's not true. I'm her biggest fan." Owen took her hands. "You got to hang on, Honeybear. Only a few more treatments and you'll be finished. Then we'll go see Lia in concert, okay?"

"I'm just so tired." Kylie reached over and wiped a tear off Owen's face. "I don't need Lia Castaneda any more. I've got you."

"Then please say you'll keep fighting for me, okay? Because I don't want you to give up." He held her hands.

Kylie gave a half smile. "I guess I can try a bit more for you."

"That's good, Honeybear." He looked up.

Everyone was standing around, looking like they were trying not to cry. Poet felt Abby's hands on her shoulders.

"Look Honeybear, it's the Jellybean Man. Maybe he can give you a jellybean," Owen said.

"I think we can do better than that," Lia said, wiping her face and then taking off her wig. "Kylie, sorry, I didn't get your picture. But Tessa thought you were so lovely she wanted me to meet you. I'm so glad I came."

Owen, who'd be squatting down, fell on his butt on the ground.

Lucky he had jeans on underneath his hospital gown.

Kylie's hands were over her mouth but for a sick girl she could still scream loud.

Then she started thumping Owen on the shoulder.

Not that it would've hurt. She looked so weak it probably felt like a butterfly bumped into him.

"It's Lia, it's Lia, it's Lia Castaneda!" she said not taking her eyes off Lia. "How did you do this, Owen?"

"I didn't Kylie. I think it's magic."

"Maybe fairy tales are real," Kylie whispered, turning her face and then her eyes to Owen.

Owen smiled. "Maybe, Kylie Honeybear. Maybe they are."

"I've just got to get Dakota and a few other girls," the nurse said. "They'll so want to meet you, Ms Castaneda. Will that be okay?"

"Sure," Lia said.

"Please don't let anyone else know Lia's here," Andrew said.

"My lips are sealed," the nurse said.

What about the Fireman? Maybe Andrew should go with the nurse to make sure she didn't tell anyone Lia was here.

Poet looked over to Andrew. He was standing very close to Tessa and they were whispering to each other with goopy-looking faces.

If that's how love made your face go, she didn't want anything to do with it. No way! Guess she'd have to stop thinking about Brody. She looked at Brody and sighed.

"Really?" Nate said, looking at her, then at Brody. "Could this day get any crazier?"

Chapter Twenty-six:
Taken

Early Sunday Afternoon

Nate was hungry. Hadn't Tessa said something about meat pies? He'd love a meat pie right now.

Lia and the Jellybean Man were entertaining a bunch of kids. Mum, Dad, and Owen were each sitting with a child on their lap, munching on jellybeans. Brody, Logan, Poet, and Meeka were joking around with a couple of other kids. Poet couldn't take her eyes off Brody.

Major crush. Nate couldn't wait to tease her about it.

Andrew had left to talk to the police and do security stuff. Probably looking for his Captain America shield. Or his Quasimodo bells. Maybe he was having an identity crisis.

"Hey, Cole," Nate said. "Shall we go find some food? Tessa mentioned something about meat pies."

"I am hungry, but I don't think we're supposed to leave."

"Did someone say meat pies?" Tessa asked, putting her pencil down. She'd been making outlines of a crocodile on the wall next to the picture of Lia. Very cool. Maybe she'd do a motorbike next.

"Miss Cowan?" Nate said.

"Please, call me Tessa. Miss Cowan isn't my name."

"Tessa, you could have the crocodile sitting on a motorbike."

Tessa and Cole stared at the mural.

"You any good at motorbikes, Cole?" she asked.

"Not too bad. Drawn lots of dirt bikes for Logan. Could easily change it into something flashier."

"Let's do that. But first, we should get some meat pies. It's only down the lift on the ground floor, so it should be safe. It's crowded at this time."

She stepped over to the door and pushed it open a bit. "Sergeant Scary's there. We'll get him to come with us and we'll be fine."

"Sounds good. How about I stay here and start outlining the motorbike? I'll have to rub out your crocodile though," Cole said.

"No problem. Let's go, Nate," she said.

No one else was in the hall. Sergeant Scary was standing by the lift.

"Going somewhere?" he asked Tessa.

"To the café to get some pies," she said. "We figured we'll be safe if you come with us."

"Of course," Sergeant Scary said.

They waited for the lift to arrive.

"I'm sorry about the laxative in the lemonade," Tessa said.

Sergeant Scary stared at her. He looked big and muscled and kind of dangerous. Tessa sure was brave to muck around with him.

"All is forgiven, Tessa," he said.

The lift doors opened and they went in, Sergeant Scary between them. The doors shut.

Tessa leaned over to press the button. Sergeant Scary reached his arm around her head and put a cloth over her mouth.

"Wha…" Nate shouted as a cloth covered his mouth. He heard Sergeant Scary say 'Forgiven, but not forgotten.' Then everything went black.

Cole looked at his watch. They should be back by now.

"Hey, Brody," he called out. "Tessa and Nate went with Sergeant Scary to the cafe. They should be back by now."

"What?" Brody said. He pulled out his phone and rang someone. "Dad, Tessa and Nate went to the café with Sergeant Scary. Can you see them?"

Andrew walked in. Brody hung up.

"Where are Tessa and Nate?" Andrew asked.

"They went with Sergeant Scary to get some lunch at the café," Cole said.

"But Dad says nobody's seen them arrive." Brody's face was pale.

"It's all right, Brody. We'll find them," Andrew said, running out the door.

Sirens, Nate could hear sirens. And he was bouncing around a lot. He lifted his eyelids. Felt like he was lifting a wheelbarrow of concrete with his eyeballs. An ambulance. He was in an ambulance.

He's always wondered what it was like to ride in one of those. His head hurt.

He felt a stab in his arm, like someone injected him. He shut his eyes again.

Blackness.

Everything happened so fast. Poet couldn't work out what was going on, except she was scared. She only wanted to know where Nate was.

Chief Inspector Bankston said a few words and the police moved like lightning. They were all hustled downstairs into police cars and driven to the police station. They were shown into some kind of operations room, with computers and large screens and whiteboards and people everywhere. Chief Inspector Bankston was giving orders and listening to people interrupting him with information and frowning and being cross with people in uniforms and telling Mum and Dad it was all going to be fine.

She didn't believe him. He was obviously very good at what he did, but she still didn't believe him.

Meeka and Logan sat on either side of her and held her hands.

"I heard Brody say Sergeant Scary must be working with the Fireman," Meeka said.

"Where could they have taken them?" Poet asked.

"Anywhere," Logan said. "London's a big place."

"What will happen to Nate?" Poet asked and looked at Meeka.

Meeka's lips and chin trembled.

"Look at me, Poet," Logan said.

Poet faced Logan.

"Nate will be fine. He can look after himself. Remember how he got free from Oscar?"

Poet nodded. Nate was a good fighter. So how could he have been taken? Where had they taken them? She needed to think. She shut her eyes.

"The Mellow Hound!"

"Huh?" Meeka asked.

"What was that, Poet?" Chief Inspector Bankston asked, from across the room, over all the noise. He made his way to her.

Did the man miss nothing? It would suck to have him as a parent.

"Captain Scary was talking to a nurse earlier. She said she was going to meet him at a pub, The Mellow Hound, at half past five today. She said it was his favourite pub."

"That's great Poet. Can you remember the nurse's name? Did you see her name badge?" Chief Inspector Bankston asked.

Poet shut her eyes and pictured the nurse. She hadn't even been trying to notice her but there she was, a complete picture in her mind. Kind of scary how her brain worked.

"Nurse Barnes," she said.

Chief Inspector Bankston looked at one of his men.

"Onto it, sir," he said, "I'll track her down and bring her in for questioning."

"There's a Mellow Hound pub in Battersea," a woman called from a computer across the room.

"Then what are you still doing here?" Chief Inspector Bankston asked.

"I've left already, sir," the woman said, jumping up.

"I'm coming with you," Brody said.

"Sit down, Brody," Chief Inspector Bankston said.

"Dad, I can't sit here while Tessa is in the hands of that monster," Brody said.

'You've forgotten what that monster said, Brody." Chief Inspector Bankston frowned. "I never will. Any of your kids, any time."

Brody opened his mouth.

"No, Brody," Chief Inspector Bankston said. "And that's the last of it. It's bad enough that he has one of my kids. You are not going anywhere near him. Have I made myself clear?"

Brody frowned, and then let out a sigh. "Yes, sir."

A police woman came up to him and put her hands on his shoulders.

"You can trust us, Brody. Tessa's one of us. We're not going to let anything happen to her."

"Thanks, Mary." Brody looked into her eyes.

Was he in love with Mary?

Logan jumped up beside Poet. "That's it," he yelled. "That's it."

What? Brody was in love with Mary? Actually, who cared right now? What on earth was she thinking about that for? All she wanted was Nate back, safe and sound. Brody could fall in love with a pumpkin if he wanted to.

"What's it?" Brody asked.

"Mary said, 'She's one of us'!" Logan said. "Tessa was doing surveillance for you, even though she never knew it. Please tell me that stupid wart on her face was some kind of device?"

"It was." A policeman stood at his computer. "A GPS tracker, so we could keep tabs on where she was. But Brody took it off her, remember?"

"And you put it in your shirt pocket," Logan said, looking at Brody.

"And she took my shirt," Brody said.

"Fantastic!" Chief Inspector Bankston said, moving quickly to a wall-sized screen and tapping on a few keys on a keyboard. The next minute a map appeared on screen, with a red beep in one corner.

"There they are everyone," he said. "Across the road from The Mellow Hound."

They'd found them! Poet hugged Logan.

Brody hugged Logan too. "Thank you," he said.

"Okay," Chief Inspector Bankston said. "Andrew, you come with me. We may need your skills."

Poet felt her fingernail break in between her teeth.

Brody squeezed her shoulder. "We'll get them back soon, Poet. Dad and Andrew will find them."

He smiled one of his special Brody Bankston smiles just for her, then he walked over and sat with Lia and Jason.

Meeka looked at Poet. "Brody's dad said Brody couldn't go get Nate and Tessa, but he never said we couldn't."

Poet's other fingernail broke as she pulled her hand out of her mouth.

Chapter Twenty-seven:
Nate Fights Back

"How would we get there?" Poet asked.

"The train station's across the road. I saw it when we arrived. Maybe we'll get there in time to help. You never know," Logan said.

Meeka and Logan were crazy. But it sure beat sitting around here.

"Okay," Poet said. "How do we get away from all the adults?"

Cole took a step towards them. Had he heard them?

"I'd need to come with you," Cole said. "Or you won't make it out of the building."

They all stared at him. Wasn't he supposed to be responsible? He was almost seventeen, almost a grown-up.

"Someone's got to look after you guys. And I can't bear the thought of Nate being hurt while I'm sitting here doing nothing. You guys came to my rescue when I was captured.

Let's get going while Mum and Dad are outside on the balcony."

That hadn't worked out so well, the whole rescuing Cole thing. If it hadn't been for Andrew... Still, this was Nate they were talking about. Same stardust. They had to find him.

Cole looked over at Jason and Lia. "Meeka and Poet need to go to the bathroom. Logan and I are going to take them, keep an eye on them."

"All right," Jason said.

"Come straight back," Lia said.

"We should leave a note in the bathroom," Poet said as they walked down the hallway. "Or they might think we've been captured. Chief Inspector Bankston would get mad about that."

"Good thinking, Poet," Meeka said. "Any one got any paper?"

"Always," Poet said, pulling out a notebook and pen from her pocket. "Never know when you'll have the next big idea."

Nate felt as if he'd been hit by a truck. Or at least, that's what he assumed being hit by a truck felt like.

Mind you, if he was hit by a truck, he probably wouldn't feel anything. Not for awhile, anyway, and hopefully by the time he came around some medical person would have given him drugs so he didn't feel any pain at all. This didn't feel like he'd been given any painkillers. He felt like he'd been given pain enhancers. Yeah, that was it, pain enhancers. Even his fingernails hurt. So he probably hadn't been hit by a truck.

Focus. He should try and focus. Someone was saying something.

"...your turn this time, Tessa. I've been waiting a long time to hear you scream as you burn to pieces. Gonna record it and send it to your Daddy."

That didn't sound good. What about the ransom? How would they get any money if they were all burned up?

"Rats?" he said.

That wasn't right. He meant ransom.

"Rants?" he said a little louder. At least, he thought it was louder. His tongue hurt more that time so surely it was louder.

Nobody said anything.

"Ran swim?" He was practically shouting now.

"Are you awake, karate kid?" a far-off voice said.

"You shouldn't have given him so much." Miss Cowan said. "He's only a kid. You could've killed him."

He was sure it was Miss Cowan. She was using her mean old teacher's voice.

Be good if she had her glasses on. Everyone would be so freaked out they'd run a mile. Then they could walk out of here and get an ice cream. He'd love an ice cream right now. His throat was sore, like when he got his tonsils out. That wasn't a great memory. Poet had been upset—he couldn't tell her any jokes for days because his throat hurt so much. He hated Poet being upset.

Poet. Wonder what she was doing now? Probably staring at Brody. Imagine that, they'd met Brody Bankston. And he was a nice guy. Not all up himself like he'd thought movie stars would be. Lia was nice, too. People should give famous people a break. They weren't all bad.

Someone was shaking him.

Wow, he did have a brain. It must be big one because it hurt when his head moved. Hopefully Poet wasn't missing her brain too much. He must have her half as well.

"He's not just a kid. Mr Gomander told us how he got away last time. He's dangerous. I'd have preferred to have nabbed one of the others, but we'll make do with this one. They all die the same."

Nasty. He did feel bad, but he didn't want to die. Not like that little girl today. Who was that? Some girl with cancer who didn't want to keep fighting? He'd been taught to keep fighting until the buzzer went. No matter how much it hurt. No matter how exhausted you were.

"Focus, Nate, you've got to focus."

Where was that voice coming from?

"It's like a sparring round, Nate. Stay focused until the end."

That was Miss Cowan. How did she know anything about sparring?

"Focus, Nate!"

He could do this. Surely it couldn't hurt as much as a bad sparring round. He turned his head in the direction of Miss Cowan's voice. Okay, it was much worse than he thought. Man, his head hurt.

No pain, no gain.

He took a deep breath and opened his eyes.

There was Miss Cowan. No, no, Tessa. There was Tessa, all tied up on a chair.

He liked her blue hair. Maybe Poet could do that. Meeka would do it. If her mum would let her. Man, Lia was a spoilsport. When she was around, that was.

"Nate, you're awake," Tessa said.

"Uh-huh," he said.

"I was worried you wouldn't come around," she said. Were those tears in her eyes? That was so nice. She was crying for him. She shouldn't be doing that. Not after he'd thought she was a mean old principal and international crime lord.

"Don kra," he said.

"You'll both be crying soon. You'll wish you were still knocked out," a man said.

Off to the side. On the left.

"Ran swim," Nate said.

"What's he saying?" asked the man, still in the same place.

Must be standing there, not moving. Maybe he was busy doing something.

Nate moved his fingers a bit. Ta-da. There was the knot.

Logan was always trying to teach him the names of knots. That's right, their deal. Logan learned taekwondo patterns and self-defence with him, and he learned knots and abseiling with Logan. Logan would never do sparring, but he knew all the patterns up to red belt. He had the skills, just not the confidence. Wish Logan was here. Only not tied up.

Tied up. The knot. That's right.

He started fiddling with the knot.

"Ransom. He's saying ransom," Tessa said.

This knot wasn't tied very well. If someone used it in abseiling, they'd probably fall to their death. Ridiculous. Safety was in the details. That's what Dad always said. Man, he loved Dad. What a cool man. He was only ever away for a day or two. Not weeks on end. And he knew the answer to everything. Dad would make him tie this knot again and again until he got it right.

"He means, how can you get any ransom if you kill us?" Tessa said.

She was reading his mind. That was sweet. Maybe if he looked at her she'd see what he was thinking of doing when he got this knot untied. He would need help. He might not be able to stand. Did his legs still work? Hang about. Did he even have legs? He couldn't feel them.

He jerked his head down.

Ouch ouch OUCH. That hurt. Cole wouldn't complain. Nate could cope too. Breathe. Nate opened his eyes. Phew, his legs were still there. Couldn't be much of a kicking ninja without legs. Wouldn't need Logan's birthday socks either. Logan better have got him a decent present.

"No one's going to pay a ransom now they know I'm involved. They'll expect me to kill you both. This is a message to your father. I always get my kid."

"But why have you got Nate here? He's got nothing to do with Dad. He doesn't even know him. Let him go. Please."

"He's an extra for Mr Gomander. He was pretty peeved about losing all his bullion. Drove him a little crazy. Wants a bit of revenge. I'm helping him out because he helped me out. Out of prison, that is."

"You must have been so DOWN and out in prison. How did he do that? Did he untie you or something?"

That was a weird thing for Tessa to say. Untie you in prison? They don't tie people up in prison, do they? DOWN and out?

He lifted his head and looked at Tessa. At Tessa's hands. They were loose. Just like his.

"What do you mean, untied?" the man said.

"Now!" Tessa said.

He pushed himself and his chair downwards in the man's direction, tackling him with his freed arms. The man fell over and Tessa was all over him, punching him in the chest and face.

The man yanked on Tessa's hair, punched her in the stomach, and stood up.

Man, he wanted to throw up. Focus focus focus. Untie your legs.

Tessa was fighting back. She kneed the man in the groin, but he yanked her hair and pulled her off balance.

Stand up. Stand up.

"Arghh!" Nate screamed as he stood up, holding his head. He kicked the man hard in the chest.

The man yelled. Nate jumped, kicked him in the neck, spun around, landed on the leg he'd kicked with, and kicked the man in the head with his other leg.

The man fell over, unconscious.

Nate fell to his knees screaming, cradling his own head. He felt Tessa's arms wrap around his shoulders.

"Well, that was stupid," a woman said through the pain in his head.

Gillian. It was Gillian.

He turned and looked at her. She was pointing a gun at them.

It was over. He knew it. The noise in the head was like the buzzer in sparring, telling him his round was over. And he'd lost. He had nothing left inside of him to fight another round. He collapsed onto his back and shut his eyes.

Chapter Twenty-eight:
Sergeant Scary

Logan's stomach tied itself in knots as he walked around the platform. The train had stopped and hadn't started again. An announcement came over the loudspeakers that there was some delay due to another train further up the track.

When would the train start again?

"Why did the train have to stop?" Meeka asked. "We were only three stops away."

"How come you're so good on the trains, Meeka?" Logan asked. "When you visited us, you said you'd never used the Underground."

Meeka bit her lip. "Weeelllll…"

"You lied! Again." Logan frowned.

"Mum and Dad were right there at the table with us. I had to lie. They didn't know." She sighed. "I tried to run away last year. I got to the train station and had no idea what I was supposed to do. The next minute Tessa's standing beside me.

Walter had told her I'd run away and she'd tracked me down somehow. Said it was easy—I was the only lost-and-scared-looking child there. She couldn't believe I'd never been on the Underground so she made me ride trains with her all day. We had a lot of fun. I miss her. She's got to be okay. We have to get to her."

Unbelievable! What else had Meeka gotten up to when no one was watching?

"You know what?" Cole put his hands on Poet's shoulders from behind. "I wouldn't put it past Chief Inspector Bankston to have the train stopped when he read your note. He seems to have a lot of authority. Everybody jumps even before he's told them how high."

"You're right. Let's find someone to ask about the train," Poet said.

"I'll go up to the ticket hall and find out what's going on. If the train starts, don't leave without me," Cole said.

"Of course not." Meeka smiled. "You're the bodyguard now, Mr Ninja."

"There's only one ninja, that's Ninja Nate. We've got to get him back," Cole said. He turned and headed towards the stairs.

"That guy over there looks like a policeman," Logan said, pointing to a large man in uniform with his back towards them. "I'm going to ask him."

He went over and tapped the man on the shoulder. He turned around.

Sergeant Scary.

Nate lay very still. The noise in his head quietened down. He kept his eyes shut and focused on what was being said.

"Gillian! How could you do this?" Tessa asked.

"Is that you, Miss Cowan?" Gillian said. "Wow!"

"You're in a lot of trouble, Gillian," Tessa said. "The police know who you are and what you're up to. If you stop now and help us get out of here, things will go a lot better for you."

"I think not. Right now, all I care about is getting rid of you two."

"Why?" Tessa asked. "We never did anything to you."

"You totally ruined my setup at the Castaneda-Whitley's. I would have been rolling in it for the rest of my life with what I could have taken from Lia's bank account. I just needed to get rid of Meeka. But never mind all that now. You're right. I'm in a lot of trouble if I hang around here any longer. I've no time for fires. I'll just have to shoot you."

Nate forced his eyes open.

Don't shoot! Not Tessa. She was the best.

Gillian was a foot away from Tessa, right hand holding a gun at her head, left hand looking at her watch.

Tessa ducked to her left at the same time as making a grab for the gun. Her other hand came up and wacked Gillian's wrist and twisted the gun back at her, then she pulled away. The gun was hers. In a flash. She stepped forward and hit Gillian on her head with it. Gillian staggered back.

Hope that hurt as bad as his head hurt.

"Go, Teach!" he tried to yell.

Tessa looked at him, smiled and pulled the gun to pieces in a few seconds without even looking at it.

He was in love.

"Watch out!" he yelled.

Gillian grabbed Tessa's hair and yanked her head back. Tessa opened her mouth to scream and Gillian stuffed something in it, then used her hand to clamp Tessa's mouth shut.

Tessa's hands reached for her own throat and she gagged.

Gillian ran out the door.

Tessa started gasping for breath and staggering.

Chocolate. Gillian had given her chocolate. She must've known about Tessa's allergy to chocolate.

Tessa was lying on the floor beside Nate, shaking. Her whole face had swollen up.

He had to find her EpiPen.

He sat up and reached into her skirt pocket. There it was.

His head. His head. It was going to explode.

No pain, No gain.

He reached into her pocket and pulled the EpiPen out.

What was he supposed to do with it? He could barely lift his arm, everything hurt so much.

"Give me that, Nate," a voice said. Andrew. It was Andrew. He was saving the day. Again.

Andrew took the pen and stabbed it into Tessa's leg. Then he put her head in his lap. "Come on Tessa, Come on. Don't you die on me. I only just found out how great you are."

Tessa gasped and sat up, then fell back down again.

Cheers. There were cheers.

Nate looked around. There were a whole bunch of police with guns, standing around and cheering.

Two of them were holding Gillian, while another two had the Fireman between them.

It was all going to be okay.

"Make way for the paramedics," he heard someone say. He shut his eyes again.

They shot open.

"What about Sergeant Scary?" he asked.

Logan couldn't believe his eyes. It was Sergeant Scary.

"You! Get out of my way." Sergeant Scary grabbed Logan's shoulders. He was going to push Logan onto the tracks!

Logan thrust the heel of his palm into Sergeant Scary's nose. His head snapped backwards. Before Sergeant Scary could react, Logan grabbed Sergeant Scary's head and brought his knee hard up into Sergeant Scary's chin, pushing his head back again. Next, Logan pulled his hand back and rammed his fingertips into Sergeant Scary's throat.

Sergeant Scary gagged and fell backwards clutching his neck.

Chaos erupted. There were police officers running towards them down the stairs. They grabbed Sergeant Scary and had him cuffed in less than thirty seconds.

Logan was shaking. How had he done that? He hadn't even thought. He'd just acted.

Cole was right there beside him.

"You all right, Logan?" he asked. "That was brilliant."

"I don't know how I did it," Logan said.

"I do. It's all that self-defense and pattern work you've been doing with Nate. All this time you think you've been helping him train, but he's been teaching you. On purpose."

"You think so?" Logan asked.

"I know so. That was our plan." Cole winked at him. "You're not a scaredy-cat, Logan. You're cautious and you keep your head. The perfect martial artist."

"Thanks, Cole," Logan said. "But I could do with my dirt bike right now."

Cole laughed.

Poet hugged him. "You were amazing Logan!"

"That was battle-bout-blast-some." Meeka punched the air.

A police officer came up to them. "Nice work, guys. But you're all in a lot of trouble. Chief Inspector Bankston's not happy about having to stop the train to keep you guys safe."

Cole had been right. The train had stopped. For them. Wow.

"Let's get you to the hospital," the police officer said.

"The hospital?" Logan asked. "We're okay."

"I saw that. You know how to handle yourself. I was meaning your brother and Tessa, they're in hospital. Don't worry—they'll recover. Let's go. Your parents are going nuts."

Chapter Twenty-nine:
Convincing Tessa To Stay

Monday morning, Hospital

Nate was happy everyone was excited he was doing well
and could go home the next morning. It was like being in the
middle of a sonic boom. So much noise. Tears and
happiness, explanations and telling offs, and Chief Inspector
Bankston.

He shut his eyes and pretended to be asleep during Chief
Inspector Bankston's lecture. That man sure knew how to
make the others feel bad. But imagine, Chief Inspector
Bankston had stopped the train for them! That was so cool.
The best part.

No, Logan dealing to Sergeant Scary was the best part. If
only he could've seen that.

Awesome made everyone leave after lunch. Except for Andrew. He was allowed to stay and talk to Tessa all day. What could they talk about for so long?

But he had his own room. So quiet. So peaceful. Perfect. His head didn't hurt so much any more, but his whole body ached.

He needed to sleep. He shut his eyes.

Birthday! When was his birthday?

If Logan got him ninja socks, he'd be so mad.

Tuesday mid-morning, Andrew's Kitchen

Meeka sighed. They were home from the hospital with Nate. Thank goodness he was a lot better. She'd never seen someone look so ill. Except for the kids in the cancer ward, of course. Mum was sad about them. Said she was going to put on a concert for them at the hospital.

It was all over. Brody had left. Her crew would be going soon. That sucked big time. Would Tessa stay? Andrew had brought her back from the hospital yesterday afternoon and she'd spent a long time talking to Mum and Dad behind closed doors.

"Can't you force her to stay?" Meeka asked Dad. They were all sitting around Andrew's breakfast bar, watching him put some lemon muffins in the oven.

Yum. Lemon was Tessa's favourite. She had to stay.

"I can't force her, honey. We pretty much begged her. She needed to rest a bit and think about it."

Meeka looked at Nate. He winked at her.

Why?

"Where is she now?" Nate asked.

"She's on her way." Logan peered out the door. "She's just locking her front door. Hope she shut the back window."

"Ha ha," Steve said.

"Well, Poet and I have worked out how to make her stay. But Andrew, you've got to get into the pantry right now or she'll go all gooey," Nate said.

"Pardon?" Andrew asked.

"Gooey over those lemon muffins you're making." Poet elbowed Nate. "Can all you adults please go in your pantry. It's as big as a lounge in there. And we need a private conversation with Tessa. Kid stuff."

Lia looked like the elephant was back.

"It's not like we're asking you to sit on the floor again," Meeka said.

"You can listen in and interrupt us if you need to," Nate said. "Please, Dad?"

"Oh, all right," Steve said. "This better be good. And there'll be no adults hiding in our house. It's strictly a weird thing famous people do in their homes. Isn't that right Lia?"

Lia laughed. "There's a lot weirder things famous people do. Have I told you about Jason sleep-singing?"

"I do not sleep-sing," he said and followed them into the pantry. He popped his head back around. "This is the last time we hide for you guys. So this better be good."

"Don't sing, Dad. That's all we ask. You sound worse than Poet." Meeka nudged Poet. "Get in there Dad. Tessa's almost here."

The pantry door shut behind the adults. Just in time. What on earth were Nate and Poet up to?

"Hi, guys," Tessa said, walking into the room. "You're looking much better, Nate. Where are the parent people?"

"Oh, they're about somewhere." Poet waved her arm around.

"Are you going to stay?" Nate asked. "Everyone wants you to."

"They say that, but..." She shrugged. "I still feel like an imposter. And I'm not serious enough for Meeka."

She leaned over and squeezed Meeka's shoulder. "She needs someone sensible. Like another Andrew."

"No, I don't!" Meeka shouted.

Nate stood on Meeka's foot. "She's already got one Andrew. She needs someone fun..."

"Someone who can understand her..." Poet said.

"Someone who can figure out what stupid un-sensible thing she's about to do next," Nate said.

"Someone who can tell when she's lying," Logan said, rolling his eyes. "Nobody else has a clue."

Meeka elbowed him in the stomach. He elbowed her back.

"Am I right or am I right?" Logan asked.

"I think you may be right Logan." Tessa smiled.

"See. You and Andrew are the perfect team for Meeka," Poet said. "One silly, one sensible."

Tessa frowned at her.

"She didn't mean silly," Logan said. "I think she meant ridiculous."

"That's better. I like ridiculous," Tessa smiled.

"Then that's exactly what I meant." Poet shook her head. "And if you did leave, how are you going to get by without Andrew..."

"...seeing as you're secretly in love with him," Nate said.

Tessa snorted. "Nate, I think the earth tilted on its axis overnight and the change in the gravitational pull has made your brain fall out of your head."

"No, it hasn't," Poet said. "Please listen for a minute. You had lots of mean thoughts about Andrew, didn't you?"

"Lots and lots," Tessa said.

"Nate, remember when I told you that Todd at school was being mean to me all the time?" Poet said. "You said he must be secretly in love with me."

"That's right," Nate said. "And it turned out to be true. He wrote her a poem and bought her flowers and everything. So, it could be true that you're in love with Andrew. You just wouldn't know..."

"...because it's a secret." Tessa finished, shaking her head. "I knew I should've stayed in bed this morning."

"We can prove it to you," Poet said.

"And then you'll have to stay," Meeka said. "Come on, Tessa. Play along for a minute. Please."

Tessa sighed. "All right. For you, Meeka. Only for you. Hit me with it, Doctor Love. How will I ever find out if I'm secretly in love with him?"

"Well, if he was here, it would be easy to tell. Your brain would turn to mush each time you saw him, and your face would look like this." Poet pulled a crazy expression, and everyone laughed.

"Your face does look a bit like that when Andrew's around," Nate said.

"That's his awful aftershave," Tessa said and cringed. "How did you do that to your face, Poet? I can't get my face to look anything like that." Tessa scrunched up her face so many ways they all started laughing.

"Stop it, Tessa," Meeka said.

Tessa chuckled. "If I looked like that, Andrew would say, 'Miss Cowan, I do believe when you put your face on this morning you tightened the screw at the back a little tight. Let me get my wrench and I'll whack it loose for you'."

The laughing quietened down to a giggle.

"I think I'm safe," Tessa said. "I can't possibly be in love. My face doesn't look anything like that."

Chapter Thirty:
Subconscious Mind

Poet held her fingertips to sides of her head and spoke in a sing-song voice, "Well, maybe you're so deeply, secretly, truly in love even your subconscious is trying to hide. You need to get past your conscious mind and trick your subconscious into telling you the truth."

"Okay, okay. How do I do that, Doctor?" Tessa asked, rolling her eyes.

"Shut your eyes and think about Andrew," Poet said.

"Hmm, big, squashed nose, hair everywhere, swings from tree to tree," she said with her eyes shut.

"That's the gorilla we saw in the zoo last time you were here," Meeka said.

"That's right. He was called Bozo. Quite a few similarities to Andrew, now I think about it."

The others all grinned.

"Please be serious, Tessa," Poet asked.

Tessa shut her eyes again and nodded for her to go on.

"Now, imagine he's kissing you."

"Yuk!" Tessa opened her eyes wide and sat forward. "You've got to be kidding."

Nate and Logan covered their mouths with their hands.

"Stop it," Poet said. "That's your conscious mind reacting. You've got to wait for forty seconds for that to pass then see what you really feel."

"Do I have to imagine him kissing me for the whole forty seconds?" Tessa asked.

Poet nodded.

"That's going to be difficult. I don't know if I can," Tessa said.

"Please Tessa," Poet said. "I can use it for my science fair project. I'm doing it on conscious versus subconscious mind."

"Or unconscious mind, you mean. That's what I'll be if I have to kiss Andrew for that long. I wondered where you were getting all this stuff from. I'll try for the sake of science, but I may need an ambulance afterwards."

She shut her eyes. "Yuk."

They waited.

A smile appeared on Tessa's face.

"You're smiling. You must be in love." Nate hit the bench top. "I knew it!"

"Oh, sorry. I got distracted. I was imagining eating a piece of lemon meringue pie. I'm hungry."

"Tessa, stop fooling around," Meeka said. "Think about Andrew. It's important to Poet's unconscious homework."

"Subconscious," Poet said.

"That too," Meeka said.

Tessa smiled. "I'll try again then. Gorilla... Lemon Meringue Pie...sigh...Andrew. Right. Got it. Yuk, he's going to kiss me!" Her eyes shot open. "Do you think he cleaned his teeth? One time I went on a date with this guy who had garlic breath and he tried to kiss me. Never again."

"Tessa," Meeka and Poet said together. Logan and Nate had tears forming in their eyes.

"All right ... Gorilla, Lemon Meringue Pie... Andrew kissing me." She opened her eyes and screamed.

Logan laughed. "What now?"

"He ate one of his chocolate brownies and he did not clean his teeth. I'm having an allergic reaction. Quick, get me an adrenaline shot."

Poet banged her head down on the kitchen bench and left it there. "I give up. I'm so going to fail my science project. I should never have wasted time with that bubble app."

"Science, shmyance," Tessa said. "All right. One last try, for you and science, Poet."

"Please." Poet lifted her head from the table.

Tessa shut her eyes and was quiet for half a minute.

"How do you feel?" Poet asked. "Are you excited and tingly and fluttery?"

"Nope, I'm kind of nauseous. If he doesn't stop kissing me I might throw up in his face." She opened her eyes. "How'd I do? Am I secretly in love or not?"

Poet sighed. "Looks like a no."

Well, that stinks. How will they convince her to stay now?

"That's a shame," Tessa said. "Andrew's such a good cook."

"It sure is a shame," Andrew said, bursting out of the pantry, the other adults all following.

"You!" Tessa screamed and looked at Poet. "I'm going to kill you, Poet!"

Poet jumped up and sprinted towards the door, Tessa after her. Andrew raced after them both and grabbed Tessa by the waist from behind.

She stopped running and leaned into him. He didn't let go.

This could be good. If they could get them together, she'd have to stay.

"Sorry, but I can't let you kill Poet," Andrew said. "It's a bodyguard thing. Protect the kids and all that." He let go with one arm and started fiddling with Tessa's hair.

She twisted around to face him.

He was keeping his other arm on her waist. And Tessa was okay with that!

"What are you doing?" Tessa asked.

"I wanted to see if your blue hair was real or another wig," Andrew said, and tugged it a bit.

"Ow," she said. "Don't do that."

"Sorry." Andrew dropped his hand back to Tessa's waist. "I saw Jason fiddle with your hair while you were asleep in hospital. I wanted to try too."

Lia looked at Jason, her eyebrows meeting in the middle.

He waved his arm at Tessa. "I couldn't believe it was real," he said. "She was sound asleep. Steve did too, earlier." He elbowed Steve.

Abby stared at Steve and huffed.

"I never knew Steve played with my hair," Tessa said. "I must have been sound asleep then, but I wasn't asleep when Jason yanked it." She winked in Lia's direction. "I was scared I was going to go all fluttery. You know, after seeing him with his shirt off and all. It would be bad to be secretly in love with your boss."

Meeka's heart stopped for a second, and then started to pound super loud. Sploud.

"Did you go fluttery?" she asked, her hands over her mouth.

"Nope, not one bit. I wanted to put him in a wristlock like I do with Brody when he's being annoying."

"That's good," Lia said, her eyes glistening. Was she trying not to laugh?

"But here's the real question," Nate said. "Did you go all fluttery when Andrew played with your hair?"

Tessa sighed. "I may have. A little bit."

"That's good," Poet said.

Andrew bit his lip.

Mr Serious, he was definitely trying not to smile.

"What if I do this then," Andrew asked, and slowly pushed her hair off her face on one side.

"Butterflies," Tessa said. "All flying around and bumping into each other. How about you?"

"Butterflies too," Andrew said. "But mine are flying in formation."

"Of course." Tessa laughed.

Such a nice laugh. Oh, she might stay…Meeka crossed her fingers behind her back.

"Kiss her and see what happens," Nate said.

Andrew looked at him. "I can work this one out, Nate."

Nate went red.

Andrew bent down and kissed Tessa on the mouth, for just a few seconds.

Tessa opened her eyes and smiled at Andrew. "All the butterflies were killed by the fireworks going off. You?"

"They didn't stand a chance. There were a hundred cannons firing all at once."

Tessa took a step backwards. "That's not fair then, is it?"

"How do you mean?" Andrew asked.

"Well, I kiss you and you get cannons. You kiss me, and I only get measly old fireworks. I don't think you're really trying."

Andrew pointed in the direction of the pantry. "Well, you did say over there that you felt like throwing up in my face when you imagined me kissing you. It's a bit risky for me, isn't it?"

"Oh, that. I was joking around with the kids. If—and I mean if—I'm going to stay, it must be on the condition that I can lie to Meeka every now and then. Otherwise there's not much fun in teaching. She still thinks the plural of a sheep is shoop."

Meeka's mouth dropped open. "It isn't shoop?"

Everyone shook their head at her.

"I knew I should've used Google."

Lia and Jason laughed.

"I think the occasional truth-bending for joking-around purposes would be okay," Lia said.

"Except not with Andrew," Jason said.

Tessa put her hands around Andrew's neck and looked at him. "Nope, I've done with lying to Andrew. Actually, I've done with lying to everyone. Except when I play a practical joke on someone."

She turned her head towards Jason and Lia. "You do realise what you're getting yourselves in for?"

"It's all good with me," Lia said. "As long as you keep looking after Meeka like you have done all these years, I can cope with practical jokes."

"I work with stunt people," Jason said. "I live for practical jokes. When we were filming Jungle Wars Two one of the stunt guys dressed in this lifelike gorilla suit and hid in the jungle for four hours waiting for us to come shoot our scene. You should've seen everyone run when he came roaring out from behind the trees."

Meeka laughed. She wished she could've seen that.

"Well, that's a good one to try and beat, but I'd be honoured to try," Tessa said, dropping her arms and smiling at Jason and Lia. "Thank you."

She's going to stay! Magnifbang Galore!

She took a step in their direction, but Andrew pulled her back and placed her hands back around his neck.

"I'm glad you're staying," he said. "But you can't tell me I'm not trying hard enough and then walk away."

He bent down and started kissing her...and kissed her some more...and she was kissing him back. Yuk.

"That's gross," Nate said.

Meeka screwed her face up and elbowed Jason. "I think they forgot this is a family show."

Jason coughed. Loudly.

They stopped.

Thank goodness. Any more and they'd suck each other's teeth away, as well as their breath. Hopefully they wouldn't do that again while Meeka was around.

"What? You're all still here!" Tessa said, with a goopy look on her face. "I thought you'd have all dissolved when that atomic bomb went off."

Chapter Thirty-one:
Ninja Socks

Nate laughed. Look at that. He and Poet had made Tessa and Andrew fall in love. Move over, Cupid.

"No, we're still here," Jason said. "But not for long. Someone has a birthday tomorrow, and they need to get home."

A pain hit Nate's chest.

"I don't want to go," he said.

"Why not? Is it that much fun being kidnapped and drugged and sick in hospital?" Lia asked.

"That was a blast," Nate said. "It's just I don't want to do my birthday without Meeka and all you oldies."

"Oldies?" chorused the adults.

"Yeah, oldies, has-beens, dinosaurs. You know." Nate smiled.

Lia looked at Jason. "Guess we can keep his present for ourselves. He'd probably find it too old and out of date anyway."

"Here, I know. I'll give him this instead." Jason reached for a present hidden behind the toaster in the kitchen.

A present! A day early! Fantastic!

"What is it?" Nate said, tearing it open.

Ninja Socks! White socks with a black ninja on them. Two pairs!

"Logan said how much you were looking forward to a pair of those," Lia said, "But he couldn't find any, so I had some especially made for you. Look, they've even got your name on them."

Sure enough, Ninja-Nate was printed on the bottom.

Nate stared at them for thirty seconds then slowly looked up. "Gee, Jason, Lia, I don't know what to say."

"Thank you will suffice," Lia said.

Nate took one pair of socks in each hand. "I was thinking more of ..." He threw socks at each of them. "How could you?"

Jason picked up the socks and turned to Lia. "I don't think he liked them, hon."

"No," Lia said. "Strange. Too bad I'm a dinosaur or I might have had another idea. But I only get one idea every hundred years."

"Well, I thought the socks were a good idea. Maybe next century your idea will be better. Don't worry, my Liasaurus. I'll stick around to see what it is." Jason leaned over and kissed her.

That was Andrew and Tessa's fault. Hopefully the kissing thing wouldn't go viral. If Dad and Mum started doing that he'd have to run away.

"Okay, okay, I'm sorry about the oldies comment," Nate said. He looked at the ground. "I didn't know how to say I'm going to miss you. Thanks for coming to get me from the Fireman and looking out for me. I was so scared. Andrew, that was so cool when you saved us. And Jason and Lia, it was the best having you visit me for so long in hospital. It felt like family. You guys are so funny. I forgot you were both famous and thought of you like my coolest aunt and uncle ever. I might, you know, love you a bit."

His face was warm. Maybe even hot enough to fry an egg on.

Lia stepped over to Nate, hugged him, and kissed the top of his head.

"Nate, I'm sorry you went through all that," she said. "We love you, too. It should never have happened."

"No," Jason said. "Lia and I don't want to be so busy again that we can't see what's going on right before our eyes. We're really sorry."

Lia stepped back from Nate and put her hands on his shoulders. "We have a plan to get better at the parenting thing."

"Uh-oh," Meeka said.

"It involves Meeka staying with me on location when I'm doing a film, or travelling with Lia on tour. Instead of being home without us."

Meeka's mouth dropped wide open.

Duh. Like that wasn't how it should've been the whole time. Why do adults miss the obvious? And the socks were not funny.

"What about my schoolwork?" Meeka asked.

"It's no problem at all," Jason said. "Especially as we'll have a fine teacher coming with us to keep you up to date."

Meeka looked at Tessa—Tessa was beaming.

"You'd already decided to stay!" Meeka said.

"Almost," Tessa said, smiling. "I wanted to check what you thought. Your whole 'Secretly in Love' ploy showed me you wanted me to stay."

Her smile disappeared. "Meeka, never take a job because of a guy. Big Mistake. I'm doing this job because I love teaching, and I love you."

Meeka hugged her.

"And the travel and the movie locations might be fun." Nate grinned.

"Not to forget the atomic bombs going off at frequent intervals," Logan said.

"Be quiet," Tessa said. "I thought I sounded grown-up with that speech."

Meeka turned to her parents. "Can I really come with you again?" she said.

"Yes, you can," Jason said.

"I can't wait," Lia said.

"Where are you going first?" Abby asked as Meeka was caught up in the middle of a Lia and Jason sandwich.

Jason smiled. "We're meeting up with Brody in Italy in a few weeks. The best scary roads for racing Ferraris. And great old buildings for parkour."

He raised his eyebrows and winked at Nate.

Nate's heart fluttered. Did he say parkour?

"Pardon?" Abby said.

Lia thumped Jason on the arm.

"Sorry, hon. I'm no good with secrets." Jason turned to Abby and Steve. "Abby, I thought for our birthday present for Nate, I could give him parkour lessons in Italy with one of the best and safest instructors in the world. Did I say safest? I meant SAFEST instructor in the world."

Nate looked at Abby, with the pleading expression he'd seen Meeka give her parents. He'd been practicing it in the mirror last night in hospital.

"You look like you've got stomach ache Nate," Abby said. "I don't think you're well enough for parkour."

"Come on Mum. It's in Italy!" Nate said. "Dad?"

Abby looked at Steve and they smiled at each other.

"Parkour in Italy?" Jason asked, with his hand over his heart. "You can all come. We'll be missing you."

Nate held his breath.

Please please please...

"And being dinosaurs, you've got to make the most of life while you can," Logan said.

"Surrender, Mum." Cole massaged Abby's shoulders. "You know you want to."

"Do I have a choice?" she asked.

"You've always wanted to go back to Italy," Steve said.

"And we promise no more surprises," Jason said.

Poet gasped and looked at Lia.

Lia put her hand over her mouth.

"What other secrets have you two got?" Steve asked, his hand on his forehead.

'Umm," Lia said. "I may have organised for your house to be painted inside and out while you were here."

No way!

"And a woodshed," Poet said. "Don't forget the new woodshed you've had built."

"What?" Steve, Abby and Jason said.

"I wanted to surprise you," Lia said, her voice all shaky. "I was so grateful for the way Logan saved Meeka's life in that fire at Hideaway Lodge, and I didn't know how to make it up to you. I don't know what I would've done if she'd died."

Now she was crying.

Nate smiled. Aww, Lia.

Meeka squeezed her tight.

"Logan saved Meeka, but Andrew saved Nate that day. And if Jason hadn't put the motorbike there, we'd have both lost our kids," Steve said. "Lia, life isn't fair. You should know that. It's not something you ever need to try and repay us for. Or we'll wonder if you're being our friend because you want to or because you feel obligated. Let's call it even, okay? No more secret surprises. I don't know if I can handle any more."

"You're right, Steve. I'm sorry," Lia said. "And we definitely want to be your friends because we love you guys. Not because of some sense of obligation. Please don't ever think that."

Steve smiled and hugged her.

Nate cringed. Just don't kiss her, all right? Even if she is Lia Castaneda. Not even on the cheek.

"What colour did you paint our house?" Abby asked, her teeth clenched.

"All the colours we picked out together, Mum. I remembered them all," Poet said. "All the ones you loved. Except for my bedroom. I asked for a blackboard wall and jungle wallpaper. Sorry."

What about their room? Nate hoped Poet hadn't chosen some boring girl colour.

"What about Italy Mum, can we go?" Cole asked.

"You're going to want to do the parkour too, aren't you Cole?" Abby asked.

"Of course, Mum. It's a great opportunity."

Abby turned to Logan. "And you?"

"I'll probably give it a go."

"How safe is it?" Abby asked.

"Nothing to worry about," Jason said.

Lia came over and put her hands on Abby's shoulders. "I thought you and I could take Poet shopping for her birthday present while we were there. There are lots of great shops in Italy."

Poet grinned. "Mum?" She pulled her street beggar impression. It was much better than Nate's.

"Would you all stop looking at me with those pitiful eyes. It doesn't work, all right?" Abby took her eyes off Poet and faced Lia. "Shopping, on the other hand is always a winner. Let's go to Italy. How about in the next school holidays, as we don't have to make time to paint the house any more?"

"Fantastic!" Nate jumped on the couch and bounced around the room.

Poet joined in, jumping on an armchair, yelling.

"I'm going to get my gun if you guys don't stop that," Andrew shouted.

"Quick, Tessa, kiss him again!" Logan said.

Poet and Nate stopped moving.

"Yuk, no!" they shouted together.

In a van not far away, Mr Gomander sat and listened to their laughter.

Gillian was in prison, but her listening devices were still in Andrew's house, and Mr Gomander was happy about that.

How could Gillian have failed? It was all Tessa's fault. And those kids.

They were so much trouble.

But Italy was good. It was away from Chief Inspector Bankston.

There'd be more chances in Italy to deal with all of them. Tessa and the kids.

For good, this time.

Thank You For Reading!

Dear Reader

I hope you enjoyed *The Con Artist's Takeover* and finding out more about Meeka and her home. Keep a look out for their next adventure in Italy.

If you liked the story…and if you'd be willing to spare just two or three minutes…would you please share your review of the book on Amazon (if you haven't done so already)? If you did, it would mean the world to me! Here's a link to my author page:

www.Amazon.com/Author/KarenCossey. Just click on the link to *The Con Artist's Takeover* then scroll down to the Customer Reviews section. Click on the button: "Write A Customer Review" and you'll be taken to a page where you can share your thoughts.

And if you're curious about Cole and Poet and how they came to live with Steve, Abby and Nate, you can read their story for yourself in the Crime Stopper Kids Mysteries prequel: Runaway Rescue. Get a free digital copy when you join my newsletter here:

www.KarenCossey.com/Newsletter/.

Thanks so much for reading *The Con Artist's Takeover*. See you in Italy! Until then…

Happy Reading!

Acknowledgements

Thank you, Iola Goulton for the fine editing work you did on my manuscript of *The Con Artist's Takeover.* Your comments were encouraging and detailed! And yes, an exclamation mark or two slipped back in here! Because I was very excited to see how you improved my writing, as always! (and Peter, did you see how I started a sentence with Because? Ha! Got it past you!).

I also want to thank Marion Kirby and Melody Cameron for proofing my manuscript and finding the last few stubborn exclamations that Iola missed. You two did a fabulous job. Thank you.

As always, the advice and support of my husband, Peter was priceless. You're the best!!!!

Daniel and Amy, you're great too. Daniel, thanks for totally smashing to bits my fight scene for Logan. You did a much better rebuild but I still think it would have been cool if Logan could've ducked a punch. You're so practical; but I'll never understand how you can like Maths more than English.

Amy, my darling girl, thanks for patiently listening to my nonsense ideas and sifting out the gems from the silliness. Thanks for keeping me up-to-date on teen jargon. IDKWTD without u.

FREE Book Box for You

FREE DIGITAL BOOK:

The Crime Stopper Kids Mysteries Prequel

The Runaway Rescue

The Mystery of the Deadly Secret

When Cole and Poet's father is killed, they are left with no one to take care of them. Fearing separation by Social Services, a desperate young Cole runs away with his seven-year old sister Lauren.

With nowhere to turn they take a chance on a stranger's help, but when danger comes knocking at the stranger's door, Cole wonders if he'll ever be safe again. How far will he have to run this time to protect himself and Lauren?

Receive the whole story (in digital format)
FOR FREE when you sign up to Karen's newsletter at:
www.KarenCossey.com/Newsletter/

Book One of the Crime Stopper Kids Mysteries

The Trespasser's Unexpected Adventure

The Mystery of the Shipwreck Pirates Gold

Logan had no idea that trespassing could lead to so much trouble. All he wanted was to explore some out-of-bounds caves by himself but instead he finds a new friend and a load of danger.

Before he knows it, his new friend and he are captured by gold smugglers and left in a burning fire!

How will they survive?

And how will they save their friends?

Find out more at: http://viewBook.at/amazonstores

The Adventures of Crimson and the Guardian

A Medieval Children's Story for 8-10 year-olds
full of Unicorns, Dragons and Magic!

Crimson, the last of the elusive unicorns, steps into young orphaned Kinsey's path and life. Within minutes Kinsey finds herself battling a huge and dangerous river monster with nothing but a magical cloak and a dagger. Somehow she survives, and with her sense of adventure awakened, she agrees to travel with Crimson on an incredible journey towards more danger than she could ever imagine.

At every encounter Kinsey discovers more about the cloak's magic secrets and surprises herself with her own abilities. *But has she learned enough to be able to defeat the Pegasus of Peril?*

Find out more at http://getbook.at/amazononline

Made in the USA
Monee, IL
06 October 2020